I0693125

Eyewitness - The Risen Saints

Book Two

in the Miracles of Christ Series

© Charles A de Andrade

Eyewitness-The Risen Saints
Copyright © 2020 by Charles de Andrade. All rights reserved.

No part of this publication may be reproduced, stored in retrieval system or transmitted in any way by any means, electronic, mechanical, photocopy, recording or otherwise without the prior permission of the author except as provided by USA copyright law.

Scripture quotations taken from the New American Standard Bible, Copyright ©
1960, 1962, 1963, 1968, 1971, 1972, 1973, 1975, 1977, 1995 by The Lockman Foundation. Used by permission.

This novel is a work of fiction. Names, descriptions, entities, and incidents included in the story are products of the author 's imagination. Any resemblance to actual persons, events and entities is entirely coincidental. The opinions expressed by the author are not necessarily those of publisher.

Cover art by Barry Shapiro   https://www.shapirostudioart.com

Published by: Printed By:
Scribblers Press   Trinity Press
9741 SE 174 Place Rd   3190 Reps Miller Road,
Summerfield FL 34491   Suite 360
                                       Norcross, GA 30071

Library of Congress Control Number: 2020919537
Published in the United States of America

ISBN: 978-1-950308-31-6 – Paperback
ISBN: 978-1-950308-33-0 – Epub

1. Fiction / Religion
1. Fiction / Historical

Follow Charles on Social
Media or Join Mailing list.
www.charlesadeandrade.com
www.scribblersweb.com

DEDICATION

In Memory Of **Ravi Zacharias**

26 March 1946 – 19 May 2020

"A Friend of Christ"

ACKNOWLEDGEMENTS

There are many people involved in any author bringing a book into existence. Each of my books have introduced me to new individuals who help make that particular book better.

Barry Shapiro, who created the artwork for the cover, added greatly to this book. I have known Barry for many years, working with him first in the corporate world at a tax consulting firm known as Pathfinders. He was the marketing leader there, and I was the sales manager. A friendship grew that has remained strong for over fourteen years now. Barry is an accomplished artist. I am grateful that he took on the challenge of creating the images to tell the story on the cover. I ended up selecting the art showing what Lazarus would have seen with Jesus, Mary, and Martha looking into the tomb for the front cover of the book. I commissioned him for only one piece of artwork, but he gave me two to choose from. The second piece was what the people outside of the tomb would have seen as Lazarus stood and walked slowly to the tomb's entry. I decided that piece was too powerful to not also include. So it tells that portion of the event on the back of the book. It is my prayer that the power of the artwork might draw many to the truth of the event. Thank you, Barry. Truly God has blessed you with a mighty gift, and it my hope that you will use it often to His Glory.

This book became so much better because of a new editor who reached out to me and tackled this work. Martha Reineke of MK Editing worked to help me see the many areas that I could improve this story. I continue to learn much about the English language and communication from such gifted people.

Finally, there is always my wife Gloria who spends countless hours reading and helping me improve the story, and the team at Scribblers Christian Writers Group who have also contributed to this effort. May Jesus be honored by the work we have done. Charles de Andrade October 2020

3

Table of Contents

Prologue - The Summons

It was time.

Even across the unimaginable distance, His voice called me by name with a clarity seemingly impossible.

The past four days were glorious. The journey to get here was long and arduous. I did not want to make the trip and labored for days to escape the need. The One who called me now had even been sent for, to see if He might be able to intervene, but He had not arrived in time. Yet, once I arrived here, I was stunned by the beauty of this place and filled with inexpressible joy. The light in this place was unlike that produced by the sun that lit the land I had come from. Instead, this light flooded every crevice in my soul, filling me with peace and warming my thoughts. I realized that all that had troubled me before had disappeared, and a presence replaced the former emptiness I had often been aware of.

My mother and father greeted me first. They were waiting expectantly, knowing I was to arrive. They knew I would be departing in a short time. They reminded me several times that I would be returning to this place in the future, but that my time here this time was short. I was amazed how wonderful it was seeing them both. I tried explaining to them how devastated we all were, their three children, when they left. They went on their annual trip, collecting the spices and harvesting the fragrances that were the basis of our business. They did not return, but now I had found them. They did not need to explain the reason behind their delayed return. I knew very well the reason and the sadness that event had caused. Then they walked with me around to other relatives and friends who were also sojourning with them in this place.

We spoke for hours, never getting tired, the need for food or sleep seemingly missing. There were two here who appeared to still need to eat and who also still rested as we all had in the land I had traveled from. They were different from all the others here, their appearance remarkably solid compared to the ethereal nature of the rest of us.

I listened in awe as these two shared their own stories. Both were waiting to be summoned back to the place I had left so unexpectedly.

The one man was one of the most famous personalities of our nation. His activities were still spoken of in awe, and his story was taught to every child as part of learning about our history. His mighty acts standing against the priests of Baal still inspired many to cling to the truths he had spoken openly about. He looked exactly like the image my teachers had embedded in my mind as they told me his story.

The second man, too, I had heard about, but his story was shrouded in mystery, and he shared little more insight into his arrival here, other than to say he was awaiting the day when he would return to serve as a witness to the amazing events leading up to an even more dramatic entrance of the One who was calling me. He had been waiting here far longer than any of the others I met. He was a bear of a man, tall and stout, with a full beard, and blazing eyes. Both men's eyes were remarkably similar, as they seemed to burn with a fire that caused most to glance down when talking with them.

My parents told me I, too, would be returning here, way before these two would arrive back to the place the voice summoned me back to. They shared their expectation of traveling with me, joining the One who waited for me now, but at a different time, after both I and these two men made the round trip again. I would be returning to that place for a third time, but for my parents it would be only their second time.

I waved at my mother and father, and cried out, "I'll be back," even as I started running in the direction of the voice. I wondered whether the trip back would be as difficult as the trip here, but my fears were quickly put to rest.

I opened my eyes and saw dimly an opening with light streaming through it. The cloth that shrouded my head did not

8

block out the light. The oils and perfumes that my body had been anointed with filled my nostrils. I knew these fragrances well, after all, I was in the business of selling such items. But there was another smell the fragrances could not hide, but it was a putrid stench that was rapidly fading, as if it is being blown away even as I sat up and then stood. There was a breeze swirling around my body, and I felt warmth and life returning to my body. Every nerve was tingling as my body returned to activity.

My body was covered with the linen material used for such occurrences, but while I could walk, I could not move my arms to free myself. His voice was still echoing in my mind and came from the other side of the opening I walked to.

I emerged into the light of what I guessed must be the middle of the day. I sensed there were many people here, as I heard their gasps. I immediately recognized the cries that came from my sisters. And then I heard His voice again, "Unbind him and let him go."

Chapter One – Waking Up

I know where I am, even before I open my eyes. The antiseptic odor betrays my location, as does the crispness of the sheet I lie on, and the fact that my bare backside rests on it, while another crisp sheet covers the flimsy gown shrouding my front side. I open my eyes, seeing first the unmistakable drop-ceiling pattern that confirms for me, once again, my earlier understanding of where I am. I have never liked hospitals. For me, they bring back too many bad memories. The first was the loss of my first wife and another of the loss of my daughter. Hospitals seem to collect death. I know they also are the places where lives are often saved as well. But my experience has been more of the first. No one celebrates being in a hospital. Instead the celebration occurs when one departs from one…alive.

Of course, I do not blame the hospital for the loss of my daughter; I still blame myself, although I have started the process of forgiving myself for my culpability in that event. I raise my two arms and am grateful to see they both move, as do my fingers. I attempt to also raise my legs, and the right one moves, but the left one moves a little but feels like it has an anchor holding it to the bed. I take stock, remembering back to my last memories. The auditorium, packed with students, listening to my discourse on the topic that had drawn them to that location. I remember I was nearing the end of the discourse, when I walked close to the lip of the stage, pointing up to the ceiling, making a dramatic point. I remember the bright flash, a searing pressure and pain, and then an awareness of noise and light and then nothing?

I strain, trying to remember something that seems lurking just on the border of my memory. Something I should remember, but it doesn't come to me, and then my next memory is the scent of this room. I turn my head slightly to the right and see my wife, Carol, asleep in the chair next to my bed. It is obvious she has been here for some time, as her clothes have

11

that rumpled appearance that tells me much about the length of time I must have been here.

My heart flutters as I look at Carol, the worry lines still creasing her incredibly beautiful face, with her rusty blonde hair curving around the side of her cheek, her eyelids closed, hiding those marvelous sparkling-blue eyes that captivated me the first time I met her. Those eyes that sparkled with the intensity of the mind that drove them, which was more than a match to my own intellect. What she had seen in me, with the age difference, still amazes me.

The last thing I want is to bring more sorrow or worry into her life. It has been only two short years since she came back again into my life, after the more than sixteen-year gap between when we were teacher and protégé, and lovers, and when she became my second wife. I had been so stupid, driving her away as I mourned the loss of my daughter and her best friend, Laura. Both she and my daughter were linguistic experts in the archaic ancient languages that consume much of our lives and frame our relationship. Their friendship brought Carol into my life.

At the time, I did not grasp how providence was arranging my life. I thought I was in control, not appreciating that what I called "random chance" was in fact something much more wonderous. I failed to hear Carol, or Laura, when they shared their understanding about our discovery. And I chose to ignore their even more subtle hints about another fact I had been blind to as well.

The discovery of what appeared to be a two-thousand-year-old box, hidden away in a section of the Harridan Wall would be the catalyst for my actions that would lead to my daughter's death. My desire to destroy that discovery, and the contents found within, blinded me to many truths. I would only be as I started accepting what I had been denying and fighting against, that Carol and Laura's words would begin to make sense, and the providence I had fought against would finally begin to draw me to the truth.

12

Within that box were five scrolls that were in such remarkable shape I was convinced they were at best clever forgeries meant to mess with academia and with what I was certain was true. Of course, I had only heard a portion of the first one, translated by my daughter, which convinced me of the need to destroy the box and its contents. I thought I had succeeded. The destruction seemingly complete, only a fraction of the translation made by my daughter remained. But the method I used for the destruction I assumed also took the life of my daughter, who inadvertently had transported some of the compound I created to do the destruction to her home as well. Despite my belief of my own culpability, the thorough investigation cleared me of any fault. The investigators concluded what I could not accept; her death and the destruction of the scrolls revealed no evidence of the source of the destruction. In fact, no evidence of the compound I had used, remained. It was a mystery that haunted me for twenty years. Her death sparked my withdrawal from everything and everyone associated with that discovery. I would listen to the tapes of my daughter's voice, as she read the portion of the first scroll many times, never really hearing the words, just allowing it to drive me deeper into my own conviction of my role in her death.

It would be more than sixteen years before I would hear her words, as if for the first time. The tapes I knew almost by heart suddenly came alive as her voice pointed me to the rest of the story. I found the book both she and her mother had spoken so often of, and there heard the voice that echoed in the scroll Laura read. The blinders on my heart were loosened, and the truth set me free. Almost simultaneously to that event I learned I had another daughter, whom Carol had also named Laura, in tribute to and in memory of her best friend. Laura....

I turn my head the other way, allowing my eyes to adjust to the shadows that wrap the room in a hazy ghost-like wrapper. The light is muted, so I guess it must be nighttime. Perhaps this hospital is different, hoping its patients might get some sleep.

13

In the shadows, I see the other bench-like chair, and I recognize our daughter sitting there. Unlike her mother, she is wide awake, and she is smiling at me. But what I notice first are her eyes. Their bright green shine reminds me of another set of eyes that drove me to desperate acts that ended with the death of my first daughter.

Those eyes, residing in the cover of the chest, with the words written in Aramaic just under them, "He hears the crying of his children. He will wipe their tears away, turning their tears to laughter." Those eyes irresistibly connected to this daughter's eyes. Her eyes, which once were blank, given light and life through another providence, when the tears flowed from the eyes in the lid of the discovery into my daughter's sightless eyes.

Carol has told me the story, and I have asked her often to repeat it, as I was not present to witness what she had seen and experienced. This daughter seeing for the first time her mother and saying, "Mommy, you are beautiful," and in that story revealing that my attempt to destroy the discovery had failed completely. But the discovery had remained hidden, vanished from the sight of all who may have desired its destruction.

This Laura is unlike her mother, with a face that undoubtably shows she is my offspring. Her dark brown hair tinted purple, and the various nose and ear piecing making her appear more like a punk rocker than the proper daughter of two professors. But she is incredibly beautiful to me, and her smile and sparkling eyes cause warmth to surge through my body. She stands and walks toward me, and it is then I realized she is holding a sheaf of paper, tied together with a ribbon. She is at my side, and she whispers, "Hi, Daddy," in my ear before she lays her head on my chest just below my chin. I realize she is crying, not huge gasping sobs, but a soft gentle rain is dripping from her eyes. I touch her head, and she turns her gaze back to my eyes. "I didn't know if my prayers would be answered. I prayed you might come back and not leave us just yet." Her

14

words explain the tears are not ones of sorrow but of gratefulness and thanks. She sees my puzzled look and answers the questions even before I can ask them. "You had a stroke, and when you fell, you broke your leg. This hospital was directly next to the auditorium, and so you were brought here within a few minutes of the stroke."

I know this hospital well, as this was where my first daughter had died.

"Rubin?" I hear the voice of my wife, and my daughter releases her hold on me, and I turn to see my wife looking at me, with tears already forming in her eyes as well. "Oh, Rubin!" Her words filling with emotion, she stands, and soon her hands are touching the sides of my face. Her eyes are looking deeply into mine, and she whispers, "I thought I had lost you." Then like our daughter, her head rests on my chest, and I hear and feel her tears, also dampening the gown and my skin.

After a few minutes she pushes up, wiping her eyes with the back of her hand. I feel myself smiling at her. "I suppose I am not done with what I am supposed to be doing!" I glance back at my daughter who is still standing a few feet away from the bed. Carol glances at Laura as well, and I see in their smiles the bond of love that is most intense between a mother and a daughter.

"He just woke up, Mom, right when I was asking again that perhaps he might be allowed to return." Her words are spoken with the wonder of the providence that provided such an answer.

Carol hears the raspiness of my voice and finds the cup with the straw and places it to my lips. I suck in a small amount and feel the cold water sliding down my parched throat quenching some of the fire and dryness there. It's then that I remember the voice, *"There is more you need to hear and share with others who also need to hear,"* a part of the memory that was lurking now remembered. Where was I when I heard that voice? I know there is more to the memory, but that is all I remember in this brief flash.

15

I look back at Laura and at the ream of paper she is holding. Laura looks first at her mom, and then back at me. "I was told to bring it here. That it would be needed." Laura's words again answer a question I had not asked but had been thinking. I did not need to ask who had told her. I, too, have heard that voice. I thought I was having delusions, hearing things, but that was before I finally understood what was happening. Now I know that at times, in the quiet, He really does speak, and if you are listening, you will hear His voice clearly. Laura is much better at listening than I am. It took sixteen years of gut-wrenching doubt and unbelief before I finally understood and listened to His voice and accepted what was clearly the truth.

I nod, the understanding, taking hold.

I had heard the entire first scroll, half in the voice of my first daughter, and the second half from the daughter who now stood in front of me. Amazingly, from the time she was given her sight, another gift also manifested itself in her. She learned the language of the scrolls like her name sake had. Both my daughters were blessed with an amazing gift. I called it the gift of reverse, the ability to understand and converse in a non-native tongue. Some referred to it simply as a gift of tongues. One thing I know for sure, the gift is given so others might be blessed by it. It was not something either daughter used for their own enrichment. It had brought my first daughter much acclaim, and rapid advancement in her linguistic career, but she was most excited and felt her gift was being used appropriately in the translating of the first scroll.

Carol had struggled to translate the remainder of the first scroll, and after four years had made only a small dent in what had been left undone by her friend. From the time this daughter was two until she gained her sight when she was four, Laura had sat for hours next to her mother, quietly listening to her mother struggle with the language. After she gained her sight, by the time she was five, she was already reading and translating the scroll many times faster than her mother ever

16

would. Carol became the scribe, while Laura would read out loud the words and then translate them into English as if the scroll had been written in English and not the other older language. Together they had translated and recorded the rest of the first scroll by the time Laura was six. Each of the final four scrolls had taken a little more than two years each, using this same method. I would learn all of this from Carol and Laura after they returned to my life.

In the two years since they had returned, so much had happened that I had never asked about the other scrolls. The first scroll my first daughter had named, "The Tears of the Saints." It was the testimony of a man born blind, who had been given eyes by the one called Christ. I had attempted to destroy that testimony because I saw what was changing in both my daughter and in Carol as they accepted what they were reading. To me it had all been superstition and lies. It challenged my logic and my faith in chance, which I now know was my religion. To them, it was driving them back to another book, where the testimony words were an echo of what had been recorded there already. It was that story that finally broke through my own walls and drew me into the truth. I didn't need anything more, as I now believed. But His words were still echoing in my mind, there was more I needed to hear, as there were others who needed to hear this voice as well.

"Which one?" I ask, my voice barely clearer than before. My daughter's smile speaks volumes; she knows I am not going to argue with her.

"It's the second one Mom found in the box. Mom named it 'The Risen Saints.' " I look over at Carol, remembering the name I had seen written in her fine script on the first sheet in the box where she placed each translation. With all the computer and printing technology, it still amazes me that my wife hand wrote the translation as my daughter Laura spoke it.

"Would you like me to read it to you now?" Laura's voice is displaying the nervous energy I learned is less a

17

question and more of an assertion. I look over at Carol, who is also aware of the change in our daughter, and she just nods her advice to me silently.

"Sure. Let's see how far we can get before they come to poke me to see if I am awake." My humor is not lost on my wife, whom I hear chuckle, but for my daughter she is already lost in the excitement of the moment." I wonder how many times, she has already reread this document, knowing it must be many times. I have seen her in the past sitting alone in the room where she and her mom did the translations, and she was reading one or the other transcribed scrolls, while also reviewing the other book she now knew better than I did. She called that book, "The Source" while her translations were simply reaffirming what The Source already said.

I notice there is light beginning to filter through the window directly behind Laura's chair. She returns to the chair and is carefully undoing the ribbon that holds the bundle of papers together. I make a mental note that I need to get copies made of each of these translations. What she holds is the original and only copy of this scroll. Two years of my daughter's and wife's lives are in that delicate bundle. Laura looks up at me, confirming that I am indeed ready to listen. Her voice changes into the melodic tone I remember my other daughter also would enter when reading her translation. This daughter's tone is a slightly higher pitch than my first daughter, but there is no doubt it is part of the gift. It is one thing to speak in a foreign tongue; it is quite another to be able to fulfill the purpose of the gift, edifying others in what is being said. Like my first daughter, this daughter knows this is what the gift is for, to make plain what would otherwise be hidden. Her voice rises and falls in a cadence, as if it is not her own voice, but instead, the voice of the one who wrote the document in the first place. All I can do is listen, and hearing the words, begin to understand again what I am called to do with my own gifts. Yes, I understand, my time may be drawing closer to the end in this life, but there is still more work to be done before I can finally

18

rest. I look back at Carol and see her bright eyes and am grateful again that I still have more time. I turn back, hastening to Laura's words, their meaning taking hold in my mind.

Chapter Two - A Chore To Complete

I gaze out at the vast expanse of blue water, as far as my eyes may see, and remember. The sea is calm today, with white birds floating gently on the currents of wind supporting their bodies. Clouds that so frequently drop the burden of moisture to the ground today float effortlessly, moving toward the larger land mass, not visible from where I stand. The sun is warm, and its sparkling rays twinkle on sea's surface, causing the small ripples to seem to be a pool of sparkling flashes.

Today is a perfect day to begin my next journey. But I have been told I must record my experiences before I will be allowed to depart. It is a strange thing, to know the day of one's death and yet to be ordered to tarry in order to tell the story again. That story so many have heard, but far fewer have believed. I do not know who might benefit from my writing of the story, but the One who commanded the effort, knows already those the story will reach and touch.

My wife loved this view of the sea. She is a part of the same story. She came to this island along with another who shared an experience so similar to mine that it was natural that she would seek first him and then me out. He, after all, was still closer to where she lived. But something was driving her to better understand her own experience, so finding me took on an urgency that drove her and her companion on the far greater journey.

She was so much younger than me. I was already thirty-seven, and she was just nineteen, but the years meant nothing. The common experience was what drew us together. Only she and her traveling companion could really understand our shared experience or could most closely understand my own story.

Love is a strange experience. For me it was unmistakable attraction. As I listened to her telling me her story for the first time it was like being drawn to a

21

bright light that harvests all who see it.

She was small in stature, almost frail-like, but her light golden hair fell around her rounded freckled face with those startling blue eyes flashing with an intensity, revealing an unseen inner strength. The resonance of her voice also stirred strange emotions in my soul as she spoke her story. She remained with me only twenty short years before she was called back to the experience we both had shared before.

She would have loved this day. I can still see her running along the water's edge, reveling in the warmth of the day and calmness of the water. When she would enter the water, she would become like one of the creatures at home in its surroundings. She was even more graceful in the water than she was on the land. I will tell you her story as well, as to understand my story you should hear hers and that of her companion.

Her companion left within a few months of them coming to the island. He was called to speak of his experiences to others, and if I am to be truthful, I was glad to see him depart, for he could have been the only rival for her affections. Now, in hindsight, I realize the same providence that brought me to this island brought both these two friends to me, and that same providence ensured that he would leave, and she would stay to be with me. I struggle often trying to understand the emotions that stir one up to envy or fear and then will stir you even further to desire and lust, only finally to be tamed into genuine love.

But as I look back, I understand better now than ever before those emotions. I long to see my wife again, as well as her friend who came with her that first time. And there is the One who will do again what He did in the past. I long to hear His voice again, and hear Him cry out again that command, "Come forth." I desire, no need, to feel His embrace, and to hear Him call me friend again.

It was not all that long ago that I came to this island, fleeing the persecution breaking out in my

22

country against those identified with "The Way." In particular those who knew the one called Christ, or even more so those who were considered His friends, were singled out for special hostility. Of course, I was the focus of even greater attention, for my story was one of those realities that pointed to who the man called Christ really is. The event surrounding me was so dramatic that I was a threat almost as significant as the one they hated even more.

They thought they had silenced the threat.

Killing normally does silence the one feared. But they were not prepared for a repeat of the event of which I was a mere foreshadow. So, let me begin. My name is Lazarus of Bethany. I am the brother of Martha and Mary. I was a friend of Jesus of Nazareth, who is called Christ. I died, and was buried for four days, and was called back to life by the same One, who shortly thereafter also died

Unlike me, who died from an illness, He was killed, slaughtered like a lamb at one of our sacrifices. His life was taken in hate and envy. Yet, like me He, too, rose, but unlike me, He did not need another to call Him forth. The grave could not hold Him, because He holds the power of life within Himself. It is He who asked me to tell my story, and who has promised that once done, I could once again depart this life and return in the new life that is yet to come to all who believe in Him.

So I will begin with my first memories of the events that would become the focus of so many and in my telling. I hope that many will come to know the truth, and run to the One who bestows life on all who believe in Him and His story.

Laura's voice pauses, and she looks at the two of us with that questioning look on her face that says, "Should I continue?" Carol has heard the story before, but I haven't and that strange energy that had started coursing through my body now seems to be consuming all crevasses of weariness. I am wide

23

awake now, and sleep is the furthest thing from my mind.

"Yes, please continue!" I whisper, the hoarseness once again noticeable. Carol again picks up the cup with the straw, and once again I take a long drink, letting the cooling liquid once again to flow down my throat. Laura nods, waiting for me to finish my drink, and returns to the pages. She lifts the page just completed laying it carefully on top of the other pages she has already read and continues.

Chapter Three - Bethany of Judea

My first memory of the village of my birth and of most of my young life was that it was bright and dusty. It seldom rained in the village, unlike the island I now live on. Water was always at a premium, and my mother would often make the trek to the spring of water that fed both the pool at Siloam, which was closer to the great city, and another smaller pool closer to Bethany.

I was the firstborn of Joseph and Ester. They, too, had been born in this village, as had their parents. The village is only a half-day walk to the great city known as the City of David and also called Jerusalem. The southernmost wall of that city was closest to Bethany, but the main entry to the city is still another half-hour walk. My village is on the descent from the city, just outside the grove called the Mount of Olives.

Olive trees and other fruit-bearing trees are scattered throughout the area. For a young man, the ascent from Bethany to Jerusalem is an easy walk, but for the old and for families, that final incline can be a challenge. There are a series of Psalms in our holy book that we would sing to make the ascent easier and the effort feel less. There was something comforting about those words that made the ascent and the final arrival at the city gate less of a labor. Instead, the words would drive us forward with the anticipation of arriving at the destination.

Even being this close to the temple and the great city, my family would make that journey only a few more times each year than those who made the annual pilgrimage during our most sacred of festivals. We would typically gather with others in our village every Sabbath day, where when I was old enough, I would hear of the history and promises made to our people by our God. Of course, my father would speak often of those promises when we would take our own meals during the week. It

25

was one of my favorite parts of mealtimes, when my father, and sometimes my mother, would recount the history of our people, and the experiences those people had with the God who is always there.

Frankly, as a young boy, I wondered where this God was, as it appeared He had been silent for many years. The presence of the Romans was a constant reminder of His noticeable absence, or so I thought at the time. I understood the longing of so many of my other friends for His presence and for a better time than what I was growing up in. Now I know that every event, every age, was designed exactly according the purposes of the God I now understand had always been present, even when I doubted.

I was born during the reign of Caesar Augustus, the Roman emperor and leader of those who conquered and then occupied our land. Herod was king over our land, a political appointee designated by the emperor as our apparent political leader. Of course, there is much more to that story, but you can learn of those relationships elsewhere. But the dating of my arrival is important, as it places me in the midst of a special time, one foretold by our prophets of old, and for many, a time where we thought we would once again ascend to political power. We did not realize then, that there is power far greater than position in this world, but we had much to learn, and the Christ came to teach us about what is real.

My parents worked hard and were successful in their business dealings. My father was a merchant of spices, oils, and perfumes, and from time to time also sold the freshly pressed olive oil for which our region was known. Like so many sons he had learned his trade from his father, but unlike his father he had been able to expand his business far beyond the dusty confines of Bethany. His success gave both me and my family an advantage of position based on his financial means. He had bought one of the larger stone homes on the main

26

path through the village and had paid to have a deep pit dug in the corner of the structure, where he would store the water my mother would bring from the nearby spring. The size of our eating area made it easy to host large gatherings, and our cooking area afforded ample opportunity to provide the large gatherings with plenty of nourishment.

The location of our home provided my parents with the ability to market their wares to the many who would pass through our village on their way either to or from the great city. Often, the cool water drawn forth from our deep pit, would also refresh those making the long journey. My parents told me of the arrival of one couple, bringing their firstborn son to the great city, as was commanded by the prophets. It was said that "every firstborn male that opens the womb shall be called holy to the Lord." So it was, while I was yet in my mother's womb, that my family first met the parents of the child who would be called the Christ. Later, when I was born, my parents would make the same journey to the temple and present me also as one holy to the Lord. It is still a marvel to me; how different our paths would be and yet how intertwined His walk and my life was and still is.

The relationship between our families would be a long and friendly relationship. Every year when they would make the journey to Jerusalem from Nazareth, they would stop to visit with us. That trip from Nazareth was more than seven days travel each way. On that first visit, it was my parents' natural friendliness and the offer of the cool water that persuaded the family of Joseph, Mary, and Jesus to stop for a short rest before making the final trek to the city. My mother would remember a strange fluttering in her womb, as if I were already aware of the young child whom Mary carried in her arms. We would learn of another relative of that family, whose unborn son literally jumped for joy within her womb when Mary

27

had visited her while both were still carrying unborn children.

So, I was little less than six months younger than Mary's son, and it was during those yearly visits that my friendship with Jesus began. My two sisters, Martha and Mary, were born to my parents roughly one year apart. Each of my sisters also was a great delight to my parents and became my closest friends as well. Each of their life stories would also be intertwined with Jesus's, and it was this close relationship that would bring both our greatest joys and most grievous sorrows to the forefront.

Another feature of our little village was the slight ledge across from our home, where many of the less fortunate would gather to beg for the offerings that would support their own lives. With the almost daily flow of pilgrims to the great city, our small village was home to many who would look to the generosity of those headed to the city for their substance. It would be here that my sister Mary would meet Cain, the young boy born blind, who would later receive his eyes in arguably the second-greatest miracle the Christ would perform. It was also here that Simon, a relatively rich man stricken with the dreaded scourge of leprosy, would also meet the Christ and be healed. It still amazes me how the providence that brought all of these people together at this time, would so influence my life and the lives of those in my family.

That strange providence was demonstrated most clearly to me for the first time when Jesus and his family came to the temple to celebrate not only the great festival, but also the acknowledgment of Jesus as a full member of the community of faith. Up until that visit we had often spoken, but the way children often would. Jesus liked to run and play with me and was particularly fond of several of the others who lived in the village. What set him apart even at an early age was his attentiveness during the recounting of the history of our people at the meals he and his parents would sometimes

28

share with my family. There was something uniquely disquieting about the questions he would ask of both my father and his during those times of reflection His questions always seemed to illicit even deeper discussion about the historical facts and meanings.

I was only twelve, still a year away from my own arrival at the age of maturity in our community when Jesus arrived for the annual visit to the temple. By this time my sister Mary had already befriended the blind boy Cain. I witnessed her first interaction with that young, damaged boy who was only nine when my sister had just turned ten just a few months earlier. Cain had just joined the group of beggars at the perch across from our home when a group of young ruffians, led by much bigger boy named Barabbas, hadaccosted the beggars.

Cain had challenged the group, only to find himself doubled over and face down from a viscous attack he could not have seen coming, and of which he had no prior experience to prepare himself for. My father had quickly come to the young man's aid, but not before Mary had already yelled at the ruffians. I still can hear her words, "God sees what you are doing..." Those words had stopped the attack, and after they had left, she had walked over and helped Cain back to his feet. Mary was always far more spiritually minded than either I or Martha, although I believe now, we have all matured to the same spiritual understanding. Mary just got there a lot quicker than we did.

Even as Martha and I ran to be with our father, I noticed a subtle change in Mary, and an even greater change in Cain. I did not fully comprehend what was happening then, but in hindsight I now know the same providence that would draw my wife to me was at work drawing my sister toward Cain.

Several months later, Jesus arrived for their annual pilgrimage to the city for the festival. Before he and his parents had stopped briefly at our home, but then had

29

continued on to the city quickly, as this was the first year Jesus would be able to fully participate in the celebration, taking his place beside his father instead of having to sit with his mother in the area where the women and children would wait.

I would also make my way to the city with my family later in the day. It was as we were preparing to go home that Jesus found me, with Cain in tow, and asked me to guide Cain home. I thought at the time that Jesus was returning to find his parents and to begin the long journey home to Nazareth, but I would discover later he had returned to the temple, and would spend two full days listening to, questioning, and responding to the questions of the learned teachers there. Joseph and Mary had stopped by our home briefly, desperately hoping that perhaps their son was with us. When they discovered he wasn't, they had continued to the city to search. Apparently, it would be my recounting of my earlier meeting with Jesus and Cain that would spark some hope in their search for Jesus in the city. But the city would fill up with more than a million visitors, coming from all corners of the world.

I can imagine his parents' fear and upset at having left their son in the city, both assuming he was with the other parent. While he was now considered a full member of the community, he was still only a young man, and now he was lost. It would be much later that his mother would share the rest of the story of that day with us. It would be after my parents had died, as well as his father, and after both he and I had experienced that most fearful experience as well. It would be another part of the coming together of the amazing story, and the revelation of who he really was. His mother would tell us his words, already over twenty years in the past, when he said, "Did you not know, I would be in my father's house?"

Those twenty years would pass quickly, and much would happen in all our lives. My story is wrapped up in the details of those years, with so much happening it *is hard to know what to recount, and what to leave unsaid. But since so much of my story is about death, I think it best that I talk now about the death of my parents, and the effect that had on my family.*

Once again Laura stops her reading, and at that moment I realize someone else has been in the room listening. I look over to see my friend Dr. Louis Belton standing at the door, surveying what has been happening.

His smile is broad as he approaches the bed, taking my hand and saying, "Welcome back, Rubin." Louis has been my friend for more than sixty years. He long ago retired as the chief of surgery at this hospital, but seeing him in that familiar white frock alerts me that he still has substantial pull in this hospital, even though he, too, is over ninety years old. Louis is not as tall as he was when he was younger, but he gained his nickname "Stork" from more than just his incredible height. His long thin arms remain an amazing sight, and his incredible dexterity with his hands and fingers along with his impressive intelligence has earned him many accolades during his career.

He smiles at both Carol and Laura, but his focus is on me. I know I am about to undergo his formidable scrutiny, and I endure as patiently as possible all his questions, poking, and probing.

He has just finished his review when another man, the current head of surgery, Dr. Jeremey Baine arrives as well in the room. Dr. Baine greets Louis with the courtesy and respect everyone showers on Louis, but then gets down to business. Together they review everything Louis has learned, but once again I am subjected to another review to satisfy Louis's replacement. Finally, it is Dr. Baine who announces, "We are going to do another CAT scan and a few other tests to see if there are other lingering effects from your stroke. The nurses will be here shortly to prep

31

you for those procedures." Turning to Carol and Laura, he says, "You can stay here, or wait in the waiting area, but he will likely be out of the room for a few hours. Perhaps you should go grab breakfast while he is being examined?" I notice the light is now streaming in through the only window in the room. It had been dark when Laura started her reading.

Dr. Baine seems to not notice the papers Laura is holding, and only after he has left the room does Louis make a comment indicating that he noticed and had heard some portion of the story. "Laura, what you are reading sounds familiar. What is it that you are reading to your father?"

His question needs an answer, and at that moment I understand a little more what the "task" might be that is still waiting for me to complete. "It is the story of Lazarus of Bethany, the one whom Jesus raised from death," I said, my voice stronger than it has been the last few times I chose to use it.

"Interesting," Louis replies. "I don't remember some of those parts of the story." His statement both a question and an observation. "Perhaps I can sit in and listen to more of the story?" he says as two nurses arrive to prepare me for the next poking and prodding.

"Yes." I hear both my voice and Laura's responding simultaneously.

Louis laughs, looking at us both. "I feel like I might have just been tag teamed!" Louis says.

To that I reply, "Might be," as the two nurses roll my bed past Louis and out into the corridor.

32

Chapter Four – Cart Buddies

If you have never had the experience of being pushed in a hospital bed on the way to this test or that test, and in my case a CT scan, you have missed out on another real experience of providence. First off, let me tell you, you are not in control. If you are fortunate, your nurse or nurses will ensure that you do not collide with anything or anyone while you are being transported. Secondly, you will suddenly realize you are not the center of attention. In fact, you will begin to understand while you are riding in that prone position, watching the lights and ceiling tiles and the occasional sign appearing in your peripheral sight, that often conversations are occurring as if you are not even present. It is fascinating listening to my two nurses talking about everything that is going on, ignoring the fact that I am the reason they are currently present and together.

But the real experience of providence occurs when we get to the bank of elevators. The CT scanning area is on a different floor in the hospital, and there appears to be a traffic jam occurring at the elevators. There are at least five beds waiting for access to the elevators, and the two nurses roll my bed to a stop directly next to another bed. When I turn my head, I see another set of eyes, of a much younger person staring at me through the bars on their bed as well. I can't tell whether it is a boy or a girl, as their head is bald; whether from hair loss or shaving, I cannot tell. It is only when the person speaks that I guess it is a young boy. His eyes are bright, and he examines my face quickly, doing an estimate as to why I am here, lying in the same traffic jam as himself.

His first words are quiet, not whispered, but spoken with the obvious hope that only I might hear them. "You're old." The words are not said harshly,

33

just a correct observation.

I smile at that pronouncement. "Yes, I am," I respond lightly.

His next question is short and to the point. "Where are they taking you?"

"Oh, they want to see if my brain is still working." He takes that statement and then nods.

"Me too," he says softly. "I have a tumor, and they are trying to kill it, but they want to see if they had any success this time." The way he says "this time" makes it apparent that he has been going through this trial for some time.

"What happened to you?" His next question is more probing than the first.

"They tell me I had a stroke, and when I fell, I broke my leg as well, and now they are checking to see how much of my brain is still functioning."

He thinks about that for a moment, and I can see the tension building behind his eyes. "It's not fair."

His comment surprises me, but I understand he is not really commenting on my situation, but he is definitely reflecting on his own. "No, it's not," I reply. "But then, you and I would never have met here in this traffic jam of beds!" I try to make the end of the sentence a small joke, and I see his smile at that thought. That is the longest sentence I've spoken so far, and I think I was probably a bit too loud, because one of the nurses heard my comment.

"Jonathan, leave the poor man alone," his nurse says. Her tone is one of familiarity, as if she and Jonathan have a history. Jonathan smiles at the reproof just as the elevator doors open and several beds disappear into its cavernous entrance. Our beds are pushed closer to the doors, and it is apparent that one or both of us will be next. I act like I did not hear the comment of the nurse.

"Jonathan is a good name! One of my favorite

34

stories is about a man named Jonathan," I say again, quieter than the last comment. Jonathan's eyes scan my face again, and I see the question forming, even as I hear another elevator door chime and hear it slide open.

"My name is Rubin," I offer, hoping I guessed the question he was hoping to ask. "It was nice meeting you, Jonathan, and I hope to talk with you again!" I watch his bed being pushed into the elevator.

Apparently, we are not going to be together on this trip, but just then I hear Jonathan's nurse call out to one of mine. "Rose, there's enough room for your bed as well. We're both going to CAT scan; might as well come along."

Soon my bed is even closer to Jonathan's, and our eyes must not be more than a foot apart. I see Jonathan once again studying my face.

I smile at him and say, "Hi, my name is Rubin, and you are?"

He sees my smile, and he knows I am playing with him. He finally gives me a genuine toothy smile. "It's nice to meet you again, Rubin!" I see his face change as pain suddenly fills his eyes, and he turns his head away. "I'm going to be sick," he says loud enough for his nurse to hear. The next few moments are filled with confusion and activity, as the elevator jerks to a stop, the doors open, and my nurses quickly push my bed out even as I hear Jonathan retching in his.

I don't get to hear exactly what is happening with Jonathan, but another nurse hurries by my bed toward the elevator, even as my two nurses are speedily pushing my bed along the hall. I try to watch, but the angle was wrong. However, I do see the chart hanging from the end of his bed, and his name is printed large there. Jonathan Baine is the name on the chart cover.

35

I know that Baine is not an unusual last name, but I think about Jonathan's eyes and their similarity to another set of eyes I have watched closely as I was being examined. I have a suspicion that I am once again witnessing the working out of a master plan. I say a silent prayer for Jonathan, asking that I might understand the purpose for this meeting which was not planned for by me, but that was obviously meant to be. "Lord, be with Jonathan. Help him through this test, and give me the wisdom to figure out what you want me to do for him."

Rose and my other nurse disappear as soon as they slide me into the room just outside the scanning room. I repeat that prayer several times over the course of the next two hours as I await my turn being slid into the "tube" as I refer to the CT scanner.

I spend some of the time thinking what it must be like to be young and to have such a cruel providence handed to someone with what appeared to be a full lifetime ahead of him. I understand his "It's not fair" even better the more I consider it from his perspective. I think back over my life and realize how free of health concerns my life has been. I realize I never really understood how remarkably unchallenged my life had been, up to the death of my first wife.

Finally, an older nurse appears and unlike the former nurses, takes an interest in me. She is slightly plump, but has beautiful brown eyes, and her hair is up in a bun on her head but must easily reach her waist when let down. Her smile is bright and friendly, and I instantly like her.

"Mr. James, my name is Mildred Mitchell, and I will be working with you to get this CT scan done for you. I'm sorry for the long wait. We had an emergency need and had to use the CT scanner for the other patient first."

Mildred had brought the signature hospital cup

36

with the red plastic straw protruding from its top. She doesn't even ask whether I am thirsty, as she gratefully assumes I am. I sip the water from the cup and say, "Thank you." She nods acceptance of the gratefulness. "Was it Jonathan Baine?" I ask.

"You've met Jonathan?" she answers and then continues. "Yes, it was Jonathan. That poor boy has gone through more tests and treatments than any patient I have ever worked with." Her voice is a wonderful mixture of Welsh and English accent, and the words are musical in their delivery.

"How is he?" I ask. Mildred stops for a moment, I watch as her face reflects what I suspect is going on in her mind. She is considering whether answering would cross a line she should not cross, but then shrugs off her concern, and steps across the line. "Not good. I am afraid we are going to lose him, despite everything. It's not fair, such a nice young boy. It's just not fair."

There it was again, that word...fair.

I understand the feeling, especially related to a young child who should have a whole life in front of him. I felt the same way when I lost my first wife to a car accident. She was walking along the side of a road, walking to church of all places, when the driver of a car suffered a heart attack and careened into her, leaving me with a young daughter to raise. I remember how many times I used that word, actually pointing it at the God I did not believe existed at that time. My wife's death just cemented my belief that there was no God because a real God would not have taken that good woman out of my life. It would take the death of my first daughter, and sixteen years of anguish, before I would come to accept that fairness was not at play in what was happening. Instead it was something much grander and at times even harder to understand.

"My name is Rubin; no need to call me Mr. James. And thank you for taking care of Jonathan. He

37

is a special kid," I add. Mildred nods as she pushes my bed to the next set of swinging doors and into the CT scan room. I learn that Mildred is the CT scan operator as well as she helps me slide from my bed to the incredibly narrow CT table that is just wide enough to hold me.

Mildred makes sure my head is straight and level with the skimpiest pillow under it and tells me, "You will need to stay still. It's fine for you to close your eyes but try not to move your head. When you slide into the scanner, you will hear a series of clunks. That is normal; it is just the camera moving into the various positions it needs to be in for the images. All together it will take about thirty minutes for the scan to be completed, and if you need me, you can just talk. The scanner has a microphone, so I can hear you. Are you okay with that, Mr. Rubin?" she asks.

I smile at the *Mr.* but nod my head and say, "Yes, I understand."

"Good. I'll be diming the room lights, and then you will feel the table move you into the scanner. I'll play a little music through the speakers in the scanner, to help take your mind off the exam. You just stay still now."

I hear her moving away. The lights do dim in the room, and then seconds later I feel my table move, and I watch as the tube slides over my head and then my shoulders. The clunking starts as does the music, which I cannot identify, but is soothing and harmonious, and the process is underway. I spend the time thinking about Jonathan and praying for him and then for Carol and Laura.

Thirty minutes is not a long time, but when you are in the confines of that tube-like chamber, it is easy to think it is forever. I do close my eyes, concentrating on praying and allowing the music to calm me.

Finally, Mildred's voice comes over the speakers as the music is slowly turned down. "We are

38

done, Mr. Rubin, and you will feel the table begin to move you out of the chamber now. I will be right in to help get you back into your bed."

True to her word, by the time the table is fully out of the chamber, she is there and helps me slide back onto my bed. She arranges the one blanket over me and puts the pillow under my head before she offers me the cup of water again. She must have refilled it, because it is ice cold and a welcome sensation as the water slides down my throat.

But the real surprise is when she begins to wheel my bed out of the test room, and she says, "I've told them I would bring you back up to your room." I had assumed Rose or one of the other nurses would be there to wheel me back up, but Mildred does that chore as well. When we get outside the test room, she asks a question. "Mr. Rubin, how did you get to meet Jonathan, if you don't mind me asking?"

"It's just Rubin," I say, and then I tell her about the traffic jam of beds and the brief exchange I had with him, and then his statement about "being sick." She listens, and then nods.

"He is always curious about other people who are here as well, and why they are here. Don't know if you know this, but his father is the head of neurological surgery here, and Jonathan told me he had hoped to be just like his dad. And now it is even harder on his father, because he knows there is nothing else he can do to save his son. I'm not sure how he continues to take care of his other patients." I choose not to let Mildred know I am one of them.

When we make it back to the room, there is no one there. Mildred stopped at the nurse's station before pushing me into my room. So the nurses know I am back. "Rubin, it was nice meeting you. I hope everything works out for you okay," Mildred says before she leaves the room.

I am glad for a few minutes alone as I process

everything I have learned and ask again for guidance as to how to help Jonathan and his father. I must be more tired than I realized, for when I open my eyes again, Carol, Laura, and my friend the Stork are all here, as well as an additional bed, with a face I now recognize staring at me.

Chapter Five – What About Hope?

Seeing Jonathan staring at me through the railings on his bed surprises me, but looking at my friend the Stork, I see his sheepish grin, and I know he is the reason for this surprise. Before I can say anything, Jonathan is already explaining. "When Dr. Belton told me he knew you, I asked if he would take me to see you again." Jonathan's voice is a bit raspier than I remember, but I remembered his retching and assumed a connection between the events.

"How did you meet my friend the Stork?" I ask as I watch Louis's face and see Jonathan's smile grow even larger.

"He told me you called him the Stork, but I didn't believe him! I told him his long arms and long legs sort of reminded me of a bird, but you actually named him!" The amusement in his voice was a stark contrast to the original somber youngster I had met in the hallway of the hospital. "Dr. Belton is a friend of my dad's, and I think my dad wanted him to be around when he had to tell me about the tumor in my head. Actually, it was Dr. Belton who told me, as my dad, well he couldn't," Jonathan concluded. I see the tears in Jonathan's eyes, and I know he is reliving that terrible moment when what must have sounded like a death sentence was explained to a ten-year-old boy.

"You made quite an impression on Jonathan, Rubin," Louis says, taking over the conversation. "He was telling me about the experience of meeting someone even 'older' than me when he was on the way to the CAT lab, and by his description I knew it had to be you. Anyway, I told him I was headed to see you, and he asked to come along. I thought it might be good for both of you if I made that happen. After all, it's not often that Jonathan informs me that someone 'older' than me was here for something like what he has."

41

I can tell from the "older" statement the second time, that my friend is rubbing my nose in the apparent age difference. We are a whopping two weeks different in age, so technically I am not a whole lot older, but apparently older is older, and the Stork is not about to let the opportunity for a little dig to pass by. And frankly, my friend has never looked his age anyway, so I understand why Jonathan assumed the substantial age difference. I just smile and nod my acceptance of the dig.

"Jonathan, have you met my wife Carol and my daughter Laura?" I ask, looking their way. Jonathan nods his head carefully, as if that movement causes pain. "Yes. They told me who they were when Dr. Belton brought me into the room." Now Jonathan turns serious and lowers his voice acting like they would not hear him. "How did you ever get someone so beautiful to marry you?" Carol's laugh alerts Jonathan that his comment has been heard, but my laugh is even louder.

"That's a great question! I ask myself that every day, and I am the luckiest man in the world."

Jonathan's smile has returned, and he looks cautiously at Laura. He doesn't say anything, but I watch as Laura examines Jonathan as well, and I see the fire in her eyes. Jonathan is captivated but remains silent. At that moment, I feel something warm crossing the distance between my daughter and this young boy, something only a father I think could recognize. Jonathan is more than captivated by my daughter. His young heart has helplessly fallen for this older girl with the sparkling green eyes.

It's Louis, aka the Stork, who breaks the moment. "I told Jonathan your daughter was reading a story to you, and that I wanted to hear more of the story as well. He agreed to stay with me, to listen to the story, didn't you Jonathan?" His question breaks the connection between Jonathan and my daughter,

42

and he turns his head to once again look at me.

"Is that okay, Mr. Rubin, that I stay and listen too?" His voice is tentative and hopeful, and I watch as he looks back at Laura again. I see my daughter's smile, and I watch the effect of that smile ripple across Jonathan's face.

Oh boy, I think to myself. *This is going to be interesting.*

"Of course, you can stay, as long as you want to, or as long as no one comes to poke and prod me some more!" I say, ending with a small laugh. Jonathan's smile has returned, but his eyes are riveted to my daughter. It is at that moment I also realize Laura is not oblivious to his attraction to her. She moves her chair closer to both of our beds, reaching for the pile of pages sitting on the little nightstand beside the chair as she does. When she finally sits, she is less than two feet from our beds, and her head is practically level with Jonathan's eyes, which still peer at her through the bed railings.

"Jonathan, the story I am reading my father is the story of a man named Lazarus. Do you recognize his name?" Laura pauses, waiting for Jonathan to respond.

Jonathan finally finds his voice and answers. "My mother told me the story of a man in the Bible who died, and a man named Jesus brought him back to life. She told me a little of the story the day Dr. Benton told me I had the tumor in my head. My father was not happy that she had told me the story, as I heard him tell her that she shouldn't tell me fairy tales."

I recognize in Jonathan's response the same skepticism I had heaped upon my wife prior to my leaving that relationship the first time. I had used those same words "fairy tale" so often to describe what they were trying to explain to me. I wish I could take back all those words, but my experience now

43

makes me uniquely qualified to speak. Before I start, I pray silently, "Lord, give me the words to say," and then I begin.

"Johnathan, I understand your dad's thought, as I also once believed the same thing. But there was something in the story of a blind man given sight by Jesus that kept drawing me back to those words, and then after many years of reading and hearing the story told, I heard the voice of the man who experienced the healing power of Jesus, and something changed within me. So, I want to listen to this story, the story of Lazarus, and see if we hear in the voice of this man, something of the same. In the end, you can decide whether there is something there that is true, or if you think it is a fairy tale. Is that okay with you?"

Jonathan's eyes have moved from my daughter's to mine, and I see a spark in his eyes, of curiosity and something else. I feel that something being communicated through his look and understand. His eyes are communicating the desperate need for something to hope in. There are few times in my life that I have felt that connection. We all need hope, and Jonathan has been looking down a long tunnel, seeing nothing but blackness. Such a young person should never have to face such an overwhelming sense of hopelessness, but that is what Jonathan has been facing. Jonathan's mother had told him the story, only to have his father bash that little glimmer of hope to pieces.

Hopelessness. I know, that is what we all must face. For myself it came much later in life when despair took me to the brink of the ultimate blackness, and the voice of the blind man gave me hope. At that moment, I heard another voice saying, "No Hope, No Hope," and a different path, broad and well-traveled, lay out behind me and turned away from this narrow path the blind man's voice pointed to. I stepped onto that narrow path believing in the possibility of hope

44

for the first time, and everything changed.

"Okay, Mr. Rubin, I would like to stay and listen to the story." Jonathan's words are spoken quietly. I see Louis's face light up with a smile, and I realize the Stork, had seen the growing despair in Jonathan, and that is why he wheeled him down to my room. God's providence never ceases to amaze me. Two souls I care for deeply were both drawn here. I nod at Louis, smiling at him as well, and turn to Laura. She sees me and smiles. I see the fire in her eyes grow even brighter. It is obvious she cares deeply and knows a door stands ready to be opened. She begins again, and once again her voice changes, and the words come as if from a different person.

My father's business was quite profitable. He had expanded it to include many of the exotic oils, spices, and fragrances that made his business well known throughout the area. He would regularly take trips to collect many of these items from distant merchants, and then resell them in his own containers. He also took in much of the olive oil produced from the trees in Bethany and from the Mount of Olives, also using many clay containers made by Cain's father for that purpose. Often on his trips, those clay containers of oil would accompany him, and he would use the oil as a payment for much of the spices he would then bring back to Bethany.

As I look back on it, I never realized how much of the business touched death as well. The spices, fragrances, and oils were often used to anoint the bodies of the dead. Some of these spices, like Myrrh, are used both in anointing our priests, and as one of the oils used to prepare bodies for burial. Some of the fragrances, like Frankincense, are as valuable as gold.

I now realize my father had been teaching me his trade from my earliest days. Some of my first memories are of him showing me how to repackage

45

the various spices and oils into smaller amounts. He also taught me the uses of each of the spices and oils, as many also had medicinal applications.

When I turned fifteen, during the annual holiday when Jesus's family would return to Jerusalem for the celebration of Passover, Joseph and Mary came bringing with them the wood Joseph had harvested from his area for a table my father had ordered the preceding year during the same holiday period. The table was designed to be used in our eating area as a place where the food could be placed and served from for the guests who would be relaxing on the various cushions positioned carefully in that room. My parents' wealth allowed them to have a large room for that purpose, and we often hosted meals where twenty or more people would gather.

I still remember watching Joseph and Mary with Jesus and several other children, carrying the parts of the table into the room, but it was Jesus and Joseph who assembled the table. I watched as Jesus ran his hand lovingly over the wood top, and I later heard Joseph telling my father that Jesus had done most of the work preparing this piece for my father's house. Like myself, Jesus, too, was learning the trade of his father.

That evening, we all gathered in our dining area, and we had a meal together. I remember my father first giving thanks, and then Joseph. Joseph's prayer included thanksgiving for the wonderous trees that provided the materials for the table, and he also mentioned thanks for Jesus being given such a great gift for finishing the wood that now graced our room.

Jesus and I talked later that evening, and I shared all I was learning about my father's trade. I remember his smile and him saying, "Each of us are given many gifts by the Father, which we can use to bless one another. I love to walk among the trees and know that each one has a purpose, just like each of us do. Feeling

46

the grain of the wood as it yields its beauty is amazing. Some wood is used for cooking, and other wood is used for furnishings like the table. Some trees produce fruit we eat, others produce fruit squeezed for its oil, and still others are used for beauty like the cypress walls in the temple or for staffs to help us bear up our weight or to lift our banners. And other wood is used for gallows and for crosses. The same tree can have many different purposes, but it is man who decides which purpose the wood will be used for. So, too, the Father decides what each man will be used for."

He often would speak in such ways and would leave me pondering on what he was saying, but he also loved to laugh, and he liked to listen to me and my sisters, as we would talk about everything that was going on in Bethany. The friendship between our families continued to grow, and I know it is a true statement that we grew very fond of each other. The carpenter's family and the spice merchant's family seemed destined to have lives that were intertwined. Both of our families would lose their fathers the same year. One would pass peacefully from this life, and the other would have his life taken violently, along with his wife.

Up until my twentieth year, my father always took those trips to find and buy the spices and fragrances by himself. He would usually be gone for two or three months, as he would join with one of the caravans that would pass through Bethany and then would return also in a group of merchants returning to our area. This type of travel was necessary, as there were often robbers and other groups of people who would wait for lone travelers, to take whatever the unfortunate traveler may have.

When my father was traveling, my mother took on the role of business manager in his absence until I was in my fifteenth year. For four years my father had looked to me to support my mother in all of the

47

business dealings during his travels. It was in my twentieth year he made the decision to take my mother with him. I was to run the business in his stead for this trip.

"There are some fabric merchants your mother has wanted to meet, and there are family members we have not seen in many years whom we will also visit," my father said as he explained his decision to me, and to Martha and Mary as well.

The preparations for the trip were completed in earnest, and I was looking forward to reporting to my father the successes I was sure I would have in his absence. As normal, he had gathered a large number of containers of olive oil from our region, and I knew he was also bringing a tidy sum of silver and gold coins as well as some gems, in order to trade and buy the materials needed for the next year of business.

The caravan my parents were a part of was one that had made this journey many times over the past years. As they prepared to leave my father called all of us together. My father prayed over each of us, and my mother also hugged each of us, even though I was already a man. My father's last words to me were, "Lazarus, care for your sisters, and remember your prayers each day." He did not talk about the business but about my family and my own soul. I believe my father knew the business would be fine. He always was more concerned about each of us than the business.

They would be gone for only two days, when word of the robber's attack would reach our ears. The next day the remnants of the caravan returned to Bethany bringing with them the bodies of my father and mother. All the oil and the money were gone, taken by the robbers. One merchant reported to me that my father had recognized one of the bandits, and that had ensured his doom. My mother had cried out, "God sees what you are doing," just before the same sword that took my father's life also took hers.

48

It is our practice that when a person dies they are buried the same day as their death. There are practical reasons for this, as decomposition starts within a day of death. My father and mother had already been dead for two days by the time their bodies were returned to us. There was already an odor, not overwhelming yet, but quite evident. It was my task, to ensure their burial would occur quickly.

How can I describe the emotions my sisters and I had the first time we saw the lifeless bodies of our parents? I was not prepared for the overwhelming sense of despair and loss that swept over us. Both my sisters erupted into tears, and neighbors arrived mixing even more emotions into the experience. Two neighbors, Cain's father and another merchant, helped me with my father's body while their wives took care of my mother's body.

I had never really thought about how much of our family's business touched on death. But I knew exactly which oils and spices were needed, as I had prepared the same for many others experiencing death in their families as well. After their bodies were washed and anointed with the oils and perfumes, the bodies were wrapped in linen strips. The slashes and stabs from the sword that took their lives left little to the imagination. I was grateful my sisters did not have to see my mother's death wounds. I barely was able to finish the tasks related to my father and was overwhelmed by the physical brutality I saw in his now-still flesh.

My father already owned a small plot of ground with a cave that had formed in the ground. My father had the cave refashioned into a tomb when his father died, and his mother now was buried there as well. It would be this tomb that would now bear two more members of my family. A large group of neighbors joined us in the procession to the tomb and helped us place their bodies side by side within it. My

49

grandparents' bones were moved into two large clay jars I bought from Cain's father, and my parents' bodies now rested where my grandparents had lain before. The jars were silent testimonies to the lives that had passed, and now were sentries guarding their son's and his wife's bodies. The cave had a large stone that could be rolled to cover the opening, and three men helped me push the stone out of the way and then back into place after we had placed their bodies in the tomb.

The rest of that day is a blur. I remember anger filling my mind, anger at the robbers responsible for their deaths, but even greater anger at the God who had not prevented their deaths. The Sabbath began at dusk that day. I believe my sisters cried themselves into exhaustion and then into sleep. I did not sleep that evening. I was still arguing with God as the morning rays of the Sabbath day began to bring light to the night of my despair.

I was ceremonially unclean, as I had handled my dead parents' bodies. That meant I was not permitted to go either to the synagogue or to the temple but needed to wait seven days from the day I had touched my parents' bodies. There was the required ritual washing on the third day after touching their bodies, and then again on the seventh day. At that moment though, these laws were the last thing I was wrestling with. I left the house quietly and made my way back to the tomb. It was during that walk that the tears I had denied surfaced and rolled freely down my face. Anger and sorrow were mixed in even parts, as I continued to question God on what had occurred.

How was this fair? My parents were good people, faithfully following the God I now believe had abandoned them in their time of greatest need. They were generous people, and this was how their generosity was repaid? They would never get to see

50

their daughters married, not get to hold their grandchildren. My thoughts became verbal, as I shouted at the unseen One: "Why! Where are you when you are needed?"

When I got to the tomb, I saw small piles of rocks already resting on the stone that covered the tomb. Already, friends from Bethany were acknowledging that my parents had touched their lives. My anger with God was reaching a climax when I saw among the stones on the tomb's covering, the small cloth pouch and the clear outline of the coin housed within. I knew that pouch, and I knew the story of that coin. As I touched the cloth, my anger broke like a wave striking the shoreline without conquering it.

That coin had come from my father. It was a reminder again of his generosity. He had given it to Cain, the young blind boy who had stood up for the beggars being molested by the band of older boys. He had received that unseen punch to his midsection that had doubled him over. It was at that moment I had heard my sister Mary's words "God sees what you are doing." I remembered now the merchant had relayed that those also were my mother's final words as well.

At that moment I knew God was speaking to me. He in fact had seen exactly what was happening and had chosen for a reason I still do not understand to allow it to occur. My father had given Cain a gold coin as a tribute to the young man's courage and had told Cain it was a coin to provide hope when he needed it most. It would take more than a year's worth of begging for Cain to replace the value of that coin. Cain had taken up his place among the beggars in our village, hoping to earn enough to reduce the burden on his parents. What else could a person born blind do?

Cain had given his most valuable possession as a tribute to my father and mother. He had given his

51

emblem of hope back to my parents, and that emblem now broke the anger that had been building within me.

I picked up the little pouch and examined the fine detailing embedded in the material. The blind boy had created this pouch to carry the coin. What he lacked in sight; his hands made up for. The pattern sewn into the fabric showed he had considerable skill with his hands. This pouch testified to the importance he placed on the contents it held. He had carried it for over ten years now, and when I needed hope the most, he had left it, not knowing what God knew—that I needed the very hope this pouch and coin represented. I turned and walked back to the house, carrying the pouch with me. I thought I would return the pouch to Cain later that same day, telling him his "emblem of hope" had been exactly that for me.

When my sisters awoke later that morning, I had prepared a meal for them that was waiting. Together we sat for hours and talked. But now, I spoke of the blessing of having such godly parents for so long, and of looking forward to being with them again, at our own life's end. You see, in our faith, we believe like the prophet Samuel—death, while terrible, is also not the end. Samuel, when summoned by Saul, asked Saul why he had disturbed his rest. Samuel was dead, yet he still existed. There are promises throughout our scripture of the next life that follows this one. Later I would hear another say clearly that God is not the God of the dead, but of the living. Our existence is so much more than just this life. My next experience of death would forever change my own understanding of life and of death, but the death of my parents was the starting point of my understanding.

Laura stops as she turned the page over and looks up and at the door. I heard the same noise, and as I turn, I watch as the door is pushed open, and Jonathan's father, Dr. Jeremy Baine, suddenly stands perfectly still, seeing the crowd in my room. I see in

52

his eyes fresh tears, and in his hands are two sets of files. It is obvious he has come to my room to share news that is not going to be good news. Jeremey sees my friend "The Stork," and I see Jeremy formulating a plan.

"Louis, can I talk with you?"

Louis stands up and slides by both my bed and Jonathan's and out into the hall past Jonathan's father. After the door closes, Jonathan's eyes take a moment longer, watching the now-closed door. I had never heard Dr. Baine call Louis anything but doctor. So, it is even more obvious that something has him upset.

"Well, that certainly doesn't look like good news." Jonathan's statement is spoken without emotion, just as an observation. He obviously saw his father's face and the tears in his father's eyes as well. Jonathan looks first at me and then back at Laura. He is about to say something further when the door opens again, and Louis re-enters the room.

"Jonathan, I need to wheel you back to your room, as Dr. Baine needs some time with Rubin and his family to talk with them." His words sound like the punctuation mark on the sentence "Doesn't look like good news!" Before Louis can wheel Jonathan out of the room my daughter Laura stands and walks over to Jonathan's bed side. "Jonathan, I hope you are able to come back to listen to more of the story."

Once again, I see Jonathan's gaze riveted to my daughter's eyes. My daughter reaches down and encircles her arms around the frame of that young boy and gives him a hug. Jonathan's face is a mixture of awe, admiration, surprise, and joy as he accepts that hug. I see Laura whispering something only he can hear. After Jonathan is released from that hug, I watch as she pulls a small pouch that has been hanging around her neck but hidden beneath her top. She slips the cord over her head and then places the same cord around Jonathan's neck and slides the pouch under his

53

hospital gown. Jonathan's eyes are wide in wonder, and I see his hand reach to the place where the little pouch rests now, against his chest under the gown. Louis rolls Jonathan's bed out the door and past the still-waiting Dr. Baine. As Jonathan passes his father, I see his father tentatively reach out his hand, and pat his son's head. Unseen to Jonathan, I see fresh tears welling up in his father's eyes. *Yes,* I think to myself. *Bad News but not just for me.*

I turn, looking again at my daughter, and she answers my glance with a simple shake of her heard and, "He needs hope now more than ever." The emblem she has carried for so many years has been passed on to another who needed it even more.

Chapter Six – Death Sentences

The door to my room reopens, and Dr. Baine is once again there. The tears that had been present just a few seconds ago have been wiped away. His demeanor is doctor-like, professional in every way. His mask is no longer cracked, and he appears to be in control of the emotions that had fractured his face just a few minutes ago. He is looking at both my wife and my daughter who are both standing on either side of my bed and says, "You both might want to sit down." They both do as he has asked.

Doctors have different methods of dealing with the need to deliver bad news. I have experienced at least three delivery vehicles. I remember my friend Louis, The Stork, telling me my first daughter had died. His method was filled with emotion as he explained what he had done and how it had failed to save her. His empathy toward me was palatable as he shared his heart's desire for a different outcome. When I had lost my first wife, the emergency physician had been direct and to the point. "Your wife died before she reached the hospital; as far as I can tell she died almost instantly when the car struck her. I am sorry for your loss." There was little emotion in his delivery, just facts. It was easier for him, as he had not known my wife, while Louis had known my daughter. The final version was a mix of the first two, attempting to cross both facts and still trying to connect with the person receiving the bad news. Dr. Baine, Jefferey, has only known me since my arrival at the hospital. He chooses the second method, facts, straight and to the point, with as little emotion as possible.

"Mr. James, it appears the stroke you experienced has left little damage to your brain. That is good news, but our scan revealed a much greater problem." He walks over to a screen hanging from a wall just opposite where my bed rests. He types on the keyboard under the

55

screen for a second, and the screen comes alive. A few more keystrokes and a picture emerges. He points to an area and explains. "The scan revealed an aneurism in one of the deep veins in the center of your brain. That aneurism is in an area we cannot reach by any current surgical method. It is quite large, as you can see here." He points to a tube that snakes through the picture and has an obvious balloon stretching from the side of the tube, looking a bit like a bubble stretching the tube into a strange contorted shape. "When that ruptures, well, there is nothing we can do to save you. I will be trying several drugs that will lower the pressure in that vein, but I need to be frank with you; it appears the vein's walls are incredibly thin, and I would be disingenuous if I did not tell you the prognosis is not good."

He just handed me what amounted to a death sentence. I look over at my wife, and she has absorbed the news, and it has shaken her. My daughter is a different matter. Her green eyes are flashing with what I know is anger. I need to say something before that anger erupts.

"Doctor, can you tell how long this aneurism has been present?"

I think they must have done a cat scan when I was first brought to the hospital from the stroke, and that it is likely they could compare the two cat scans, to see if the vein's condition has worsened since I arrived in the hospital.

"No, I can't. Unless you had a CAT Scan done sometime in the past that I could check. I did look at your first CAT scan again and discovered the aneurism was present on that scan as well. We missed it because we were not looking for other problems, only for what was the cause of and results from your stroke. So, I have no way of telling how long it has been present, but as I said, the vein's walls are incredibly thin, and it is amazing that it has not already exploded." His words are again delivered without any inclination of emotion, just

56

simple facts, but he at least confirmed the earlier CAT Scan as well.

"So I may have had this condition for many years, and might survive for many more years with it?" I ask.

Slowly, Dr. Baine nods. "That is possible, but," he hesitates before completing his thought, "I would not assume that to be the case. It's more likely the stroke caused this condition or made a smaller condition into a much more serious one. Either way, we will begin treating the condition with the hope that we can shrink it, but I would prepare for the likelihood that this will become much more serious in the very near future." He looks at me and shakes his head. "I wish I had better news to give you, but this is the reality we are facing. We will do the best we can for you. I'll give you all some time to talk, and I will return in about an hour or so." With that he opens the door and leaves. Short and to the point with no real options.

I turn to my daughter first, seeing her eyes still flashing with the visible signs of anger. "It's okay, Laura," I start to say, but she doesn't let me say anything more.

"No, it's not. He's a doctor, and he is acting like a car mechanic. You're not a car with an engine that is about to die. You're a human being, and we are your family. Doesn't he feel anything?"

I shake my head saying, "Yes, you know he feels; you saw his tears, and now he has to go tell his son news even worse than mine." Those few words douse the fire that was building in her. She understands Dr. Baine's life is about to get even more complicated.

I turn now to my wife. "Dear, it's not good news, but you thought you had already lost me. This much I know, I will not die one second before the Lord wants me to, and I will not live one second longer than He needs me too. He could have taken me already, and yet here I am. So, He apparently still has work I need to do.

57

So, let us not worry about me. I need your help to prepare Jonathan for what he must face as well. I need you both to pray with me for Jonathan's father, and the message he must deliver to his son. What a terrible burden than must be for him to bear."

I came to prayer late in life. It was not natural for me, but I know its power. I have seen amazing things come from my prayers and the prayers of others. The hour passes quickly as we hold the situations we are facing up to the Lord, but Dr. Baine does not return. Instead, it is my friend, The Stork, who knocks on my door, alerting us to someone's presence. And once again he is pushing Jonathan's bed with that young man still in it.

"We're back," he announces after my wife opens the door. We all expected Dr. Baine, but I am relieved to see it is Jonathan and Louis. Jonathan does not appear to be upset, instead a smile creeps across his face as he sees my smile.

"Hi, Mr. Rubin," he says. I've decided not to challenge his *Mr.* again. "Glad to see you, Jonathan. You okay?"

"Well, I'm the same I was before, which means I am not really okay, but nothing has changed. My dad would not tell me what he needed to tell you. Are you okay?" he asks back. I am surprised by his response, as I had assumed his father's news would have driven him further into despair. Jonathan sees my surprise and once again he surprises me. "Yes, my father told me my cancer is spreading, and that there is not much he can do about it. But," he stops again, looking for the words he wants to share, "I have hope now." As he says those four words, I see his hand moving to the little pouch beneath his gown and watch as his hand clutches that pouch.

"It really is a gold coin. I looked at it, and it has the face of a man on it, and it looks very old. In the story, Laura called it Cain's emblem of hope. Is this that same coin?" Jonathan has put the pieces together incredibly

58

quickly. It is Laura who answers.

"Yes, we believe it is, but there is so much more to that story."

At her words Jonathan smiles again, saying: "I know there is more to the story, and that is why I asked Dr. Louis to bring me back. My father left in a rush saying he had other patients to care for, but I saw the tears in his eyes, and I think he is even sadder now that he has told me about my cancer. I don't want him to be sad; it's not his fault I'm sick, yet I think he blames himself for not being able to fix me."

Jonathan's observation surprises me again. I expected him to be self-absorbed with his own problems, but instead he was thinking about his father, and what was happening to him. I am seeing a part of Jonathan's self I had not known before. His heart is still tender, and his spirit is still open to feeling the struggles of others.

"Mr. Rubin, you didn't answer my question. Are you okay?" Once again, I am startled by Jonathan's persistence. I had expected to not need to answer that question.

"Well, Jonathan, your father said I have a blood vessel in my head that is about to burst, and that there is almost nothing they can do about it."

I watch as Jonathan absorbs that answer. But then he nods. "So, we both were given death sentences on the same day?" His comment sums up the situation accurately.

"Yes, I think we were," I state.

"But you have hope still?" Jonathan's question genuine and curious at the same time.

"Yes, I still have hope."

Jonathan accepts the statement. "I need to know why. How come you still have hope after hearing you are going to die?" Again, he has arrived at another part of the puzzle faster than I expected. "I know it's not this coin," he says, clutching at the little pouch again. "It

59

must be something this coin is pointing to."

"Or someone," I hear my wife say, entering the conversation for the first time.

Jonathan scrutinizes my wife's expression. "The person is in the story?" Jonathan's question is now hopeful.

"Yes, He is in the story." My wife's response a mixture of confidence and sadness. It is then that I know my condition is still affecting her, and she, too, is grasping to regain the hope we are talking about.

Jonathan looks again toward my daughter. "Will you read some more of the story for me? I need to know why Mr. Rubin still has hope."

I see my daughter's eyes, and once again they are glowing, but they are no longer flashing. Instead I feel an incredible warmth coming from her as she looks at Jonathan. "I will be delighted to read some more of the story to you." Her smile warms me, but for Jonathan, that smile lights a fire within him, and I see the warmth spreading through every fiber of his soul.

Laura reaches over to the table and picks up the papers there and finds the point where she had stopped at. This time, it takes some time for her voice to change, as I suspect she has also detected the change in Jonathan's demeanor toward her. But finally, the gift kicks in, and she begins again.

Chapter Seven – The Years Between

It would take the three of us, the children of Joseph and Ester, many months to fully come to terms with the loss of our parents. My first concern after my anger was finally drained away by seeing Cain's coin at the tomb was figuring out where we were with my father's, now our, business and exactly what our financial condition really was.

I knew where my father kept some of his earnings. There were people, whose business it was to borrow and lend out money. They would keep a ledger of money they had received and from whom, and record to whom the money was lent, and the terms of the repayment. When the money was repaid, there was always a fee that accompanied the repayment. Some of my family's wealth was stored there, but a much greater portion existed in my father's investment in and ownership of the stock used in our business. I knew the olive oil carried with the caravan had been lost, as well as the considerable fortune in coinage and gems my parents had carried with them to buy the stock they needed for the business.

I sought out the olive grove owners first and learned how little I fully understood my father's business. When I approached the family that took care of the grove where the olives were grown and the oil was pressed from those fruits, I discovered our family did not owe for the oil gathered and lost. When I met Nathan, the father of the family working the grove, I discovered Nathan and his family were caretakers of the olive grove, but they worked for my father, who owned the grove. Nathan had come to the funeral but had stayed silent about his relationship with my father. It was Nathan who surprised me first when he asked when I finally made my way to visit with him, "Do you intend to keep the grove?"

Up until that question, I had been unaware that my father owned the grove. Nathan's second question

61

also showed me how much of Nathan and his family's wellbeing were tied up with my father. "Will you keep me and my family as the caretakers for the grove?"

I had always known my father's generosity. I had seen him and Nathan together before, and I had always assumed they were fellow tradesmen. I never had seen a single indication that Nathan was a servant of my father. I spent the afternoon with Nathan and when I left, I knew the olive grove was in good hands and that my relationship with Nathan would remain as my father had set it up. Over the next two years, Nathan would teach me much about this side of my father's business of which I was unaware. It would be Nathan who would go as my representative to the other merchants later the same year my father died, where he would collect the materials we needed to keep our business thriving. In return I left alone the stipend and the use of the house my father had given to Nathan. I would later honor one other agreement my father had made with Nathan. In return for twenty years of his family labor at the olive grove, the grove and the house would become Nathan's. When my father died, there were still thirteen years of service left.

Nathan also set me on the path to understanding the other properties and holdings my father had invested in. By the end of a week's worth of effort, I had learned of the other three groves and three vineyards my family now owned and met with the seven families that were dependent upon my father's generosity. Each of the families had received similar promises made by my father. God truly had blessed my parents and given them hearts that provided for those who worked for them. They had used their financial blessings to support a whole network of families in and around Bethany and had set up a generation of tradesmen and owners.

My meeting with the lenders of money resulted in discovering that only a tenth of our family's wealth had been lost in the robbery, and that wealth was already

62

rapidly being replaced. The money my father was receiving back from his other lending was far more than what was needed to replace what had been lost.

When I shared what I had learned with Martha and Mary they were both amazed as well. They agreed with my decision to leave the relationships the way our father had set them up with the caretakers of the various properties. They also agreed with my decision to continue with our parents' business. Each of us would have a role, and mine included taking on the responsibility of being head of the family.

My parents had arranged for spouses for both of my sisters. But those betrothals were never to happen. While many fathers of other families had approached my father about the potential of an arrangement for their daughters and myself, my father had not accepted any of the proposals prior to his death. Part of my new responsibility included watching over my sisters and meeting with the perspective husbands and their families.

I already knew my sister Mary's heart belonged to another. I quietly made the arrangements that ended that betrothal. I would not tell Mary of that fact for some time, as I needed to give her the time to ensure that the individual she cared for most would be at a place to care for her. I had no idea how that would ever happen. Cain was blind, and though a courageous person, had no means to care for Mary.

As for Martha, that betrothal also would never be consummated, as the young man was killed by the Romans during one of the periodic uprisings that would occur in the Judean province on a regular basis. He had been in the wrong place at the wrong time and was caught up in the bloodshed that occurred when the uprising had spread to his village. All of this would occur before the next visit of Jesus and his family to our home. That would occur almost two years after my parents' death.

63

When Jesus and his family returned, we discovered that Mary's husband Joseph had also died the same year as my parents. We knew Joseph was considerably older than Mary, but it had always been evident that there was real respect and love between them. Joseph had fallen ill during the period when pestilence swept areas of our country. He had died quietly one evening, simply not waking in the morning. I spoke with Jesus about his thoughts, and he spoke of Joseph's sleeping and being at rest, awaiting the great resurrection that was yet to come. His voice was filled with certainty, and he spoke with great respect for what Joseph had done. "The Father is not the God of the dead, but of the living. All those who believe in Him, and in His promises, will walk with us again." His words encouraged me as I thought about my parents. I had heard differing opinions on what happened after we died.

There were two groups of opinions in our religion. One group believed there was a place of eternal rest they called Sheol and that it was best to enjoy this life to the fullest, as one remained a spirit without a physical body after death. This group was called the Sadducees, and they often rose to the highest levels in our religious orders. They also believed that only the law carried any weight in making decisions. Many of the priests were from this group, often even the high priest.

The other group is known as the Pharisees, and they did believe in a life after death through resurrection and taught there would be a time when all who had died would be resurrected. They would point to the prophet Daniel and those words of the angel to Daniel, which closed out that book of our scripture. "But as for you, go your way to the end; then you will enter into rest and rise again for your allotted portion at the end of the age." For the Pharisees, those who had lived righteous lives would be rewarded and those who had lived

64

unrighteous lives would be punished, but in real physical bodies. The Pharisees believed both the written law and the traditions passed down by the fathers were equally valid and should be learned and followed.

It was entertaining to listen to these different sects arguing over which view was true. I would live to see the joining of these seemingly diametrically opposed groups, when they would come together to silence a threat they saw as even greater than each other. That threat would come when both their traditions and positions within our community would be challenged, not by some mighty army but instead by a carpenter's son.

Jesus, as the oldest child, now was also responsible for the family, like I was. He, too, had picked up his father's trade, as had Jesus's brothers. Together they continued to use their gifts at woodworking to make a living for themselves. Every year, Jesus's reputation with the elders in the community continued to grow, as he was becoming known for his profound insights into the Law, and his keen and piercing questions. For eight years after Joseph's death, Jesus and his family, would visit us every year as they made their way to the great city for the Passover celebration. Each year Jesus's stature grew even greater among the teachers. Everything would change dramatically in my 29th year.

That year a great disturbance occurred when a man known now as John the Baptist arrived. I would learn later from Jesus's mother that John was a cousin of her family. John came into our lives clothed in camel's skin with a leather belt fastening his garments together and had a flowing mane of hair and an amazing beard. He was known to survive by eating only wild locusts and honey, and he had never had his hair or beard cut. Within our religion there are provisions for such men, given over wholly to God, and they were known as a Nazirites. Samson, one of our nation's

65

heroes was a Nazirite, and his hair was the source of his great strength. John, was a huge man, reminding many of the image of Samson that was garnered when reading of his exploits. John though came into our region teaching that men and women needed to repent from their sins and be baptized. He came to the area known as Bethany beyond the Jordan, about a two-day journey from our village of Bethany. I was not there when Jesus made the journey from Nazareth in Galilee to meet John and to be baptized by him. That event though changed everything.

The next time he came to our home, an entourage of people came with him. I had heard rumors of a new teacher who was performing miracles. There had not been a prophet or a miracle worker in over 400 years in our country. Now we had both. The miracle worker had started at a wedding feast where water had been turned into wine, followed closely by the casting out of a demon from a man possessed, and then the healing of many people with various diseases. He was even healing lepers and paralytics. When Jesus arrived with his family and a group of men and women who were following him, it became obvious who the new teacher was.

That first Passover after his meeting with John the Baptist would blaze the path that would lead to his death some three years later. But before he went into the great city and to the temple, as was his custom, he stopped and visited with us. I remember my surprise at learning that this man, whom I considered my friend, who had shaped the table that stood in our eating area, now was performing even greater feats. When he arrived, he spent just a few hours with us, enjoying the meal we always prepared when his family visited. It was my sister Martha who invited him and his followers into our home. His family appeared more perplexed by what he was doing than we were. However, his smile and laugh were still the same, and his hands still bore the

66

markings that came from being a carpenter by trade.

Martha went about the process of putting together the dinner. I was still tending to business matters outside and would come in after the confrontation between my two sisters was already over. Mary sat with Jesus and the other family and followers of Jesus and listened to him talk about the kingdom of God, and how we were to approach God. At some point Martha, who was fond of fretting over every detail of a meal, discovered that Mary was not present to aid her.

When she discovered Mary sitting with Jesus, she complained to him, "Lord. Do you not care that my sister has left me to do all of the serving alone?" Martha truly was a wonderous hostess, and her meals were nothing short of amazing. Our mother had taught both of my sisters well. But Martha was also a typical older sister, expecting that the younger sister would be there to take directions on what needed to be done. I also knew there was a unique connection between my sisters and Jesus. Mary may have been ahead of both Martha and I on understanding who Jesus really was, but I believe it is accurate that of the three of us, Martha held a special place in Jesus's affection.

Martha would relate to me what Jesus said to her in response to her complaint. He started with her name, with a tone full of affection and a bit of merriment as well.

"Martha, Martha, you are worried and bothered about so many things; but only one thing is necessary, for Mary has chosen the good part, which shall not be taken away from her."

Martha at first was hurt by the chiding, but the more she looked at Jesus, and saw his smile and the affection that radiated toward her, she told me, "I felt foolish as I knew in part I was jealous of Mary, who had been able to hear everything he was saying, and I realized he knew that as well."

By the time I finally made it inside after handling

67

the few customers who had arrived with needs, I found both Mary and Martha with the crowds of visitors, sitting and listening to Jesus. I saw all the food on the side of the table that Jesus and Joseph had made, and spent some time serving the various dishes Martha had prepared. Jesus saw me at one point and just nodded and smiled. After everyone had eaten, the conversation and questions continued for about an hour longer, and then Jesus stood. "Thank you for your hospitality Martha and Lazarus and Mary. I always feel welcomed in your house. May your house be blessed by the Father." And then he left, and the crowd went with him.

I would hear from others about his journey into the temple where he discovered the animal keepers and money changers who would provide animals for the sacrifices and exchange the various coins into the money permitted in the gifts for the temple. They would tell me of his upending the tables, and his driving the animals and their keepers out of the temple. Later, his followers would remember the scripture that stated "Zeal for Your house will consume me." Everything Jesus was doing was fulfilling what our sacred writings told us about the coming of the Messiah. It would take some time for me to accept that claim. After all, I knew him first as the son of Joseph and Mary, my friend, the gifted carpenter, but I would come to know him as something far more marvelous.

Laura stops her reading just as the door to my room opens again. There standing in the door is Jonathan's father, his clip board of notes tucked under his arm, and his surprise at seeing his son and Louis there is obvious to all in the room. It is Jonathan who breaks the silence. "Hi, Dad." His voice is slightly stronger than what it was when he had first entered my room with Louis. "I asked Dr. Louis to take me to visit Mr. Rubin to listen to a story his daughter Laura is reading to him." Those words break the trance that had swept over Jonathan's father. Even his father hears the inflection in his son's voice when he says Laura's name. I am sure that is confusing the good doctor even more.

Chapter Eight – Preparing for the Worst

"What story?"

I guess I should not be surprised by Jonathan's father's question, but I am anyway. What surprises me even further is that it is Jonathan who continues in the conversation with his father.

"It's the story about Lazarus, the man in the Bible," he answers. His tone is factual, just stating what story he is hearing. I watch Dr. Baine's demeanor, but right now there is a mask covering his face and hiding his thoughts, and he smiles as he turns to Louis.

"Dr. I need some time with Mr. James and his family to discuss our treatment options, would you take Jonathan back to his room please?" His tone again gives no indication of what he is thinking, but the lack of Louis's name, or even his surname is a giveaway at what I believe is about to come to the surface.

Louis once again rises to the task, and Carol holds the door open to allow Louis and the bed carrying Jonathan to exit. Before the door closes though Jonathan calls out, "I'll be back soon!" That short statement I am sure lights the fuse to the pent-up emotions his father has contained so far.

Once the door is completely closed, Carol moves over to Laura's side and together they sit on the benchlike chair Laura has occupied for much of the time here. I see in their eyes the same expectation I have at what is about to occur. Laura's eyes are still shinning, but the flashes I have witnessed in the past are not there. Perhaps she will contain her anger, at least I hope she will.

Jonathan's father starts, his voice a mere whisper at the beginning but building in volume like the teapot whistle as the water begins to boil.

"Mr. James, my son is terminally ill. I do not

know how much time he has left, but I will not have you or anyone else," he glances at Carol and Laura, "filling his head with stories that give him false hope. He is my son, not yours, and I do not want him talking with you anymore. Do I make myself clear?" His face is now crimson in color, but it is obvious he has tamped down the explosion still waiting to pierce the formidable mask he has built. I am considering my answer, but Laura beats me to the words.

"What about what your son wants?" Her words are spoken softly without the emotion I expected. I look over at her, expecting to see the flashes, but instead only see the gaze of concern, her green eyes still shining but her face communicating the genuine emotion of caring. It is her tone and her body language that seem to prevent Jonathan's father from going off further. Instead, he turns to the door, opens it, and departs, not saying another word.

When the door closes again, it is my wife who breaks the silence. "We need to pray for him; he is close to a breakdown." I wonder how many times she had probably said the same thing about me during those years we were separated. I recognize in Jonathan's father the same emotions that raged within me for more than sixteen years. But unlike me, he is not responsible for what his son is going through, although I know he is blaming himself for not being able to cure his son.

An hour passes before the door opens again, and another doctor I do not know enters. He is short and portly, with thinning hair but sparkling brown eyes and a contagious smile that is obviously genuine. Seeing the three of us praying must have startled him, and I do not know how much he has heard, but he is respectful, waiting as Laura finishes the prayer she was raising as the door opened. When she finishes, she opens her eyes as well and the doctor has our attention. Like Jonathan's father, this doctor is

72

carrying a similar clip board, and as I look at it, I suspect it is in fact the same one.

"Folks, my name is Dr. Browning, and I am a neurosurgeon with my practice close by this hospital. Dr. Baine called me and requested I take over your case from him. He indicated that he is taking a sabbatical from his work in the hospital due to his son's illness, and he said you all would understand. Would it be all right with you if I sat down to talk about what you are facing?"

I am impressed by the demeanor of Dr. Browning immediately, and I can tell both Carol and Laura are as well.

"Sure, that would be fine doctor. My name is Rubin, and this is my wife Carol and our daughter Laura."

The doctor nods at the introduction and sits down in the chair Carol has left.

"I'm sorry for the change in care for you, Mr. James."

"Rubin," I say again, interrupting the doctor.

The doctor nods and continues. "Rubin as you know Dr. Baine's son is very ill, and I have really been surprised that he has not taken time off before now. But I will work to give you the best advice I can and provide the best treatment possible for your condition. Dr. Baine told me he has already described your condition."

I nod saying "I have a blood vein deep in my brain that has an aneurism that cannot be operated on."

"That is correct, Rubin," Dr. Browning states. He stops for a moment and then says, "My name is Charles by the way, and you are welcome to call me Dr. Charles if you like." I smile immediately, sensing Dr. Charles has learned how to relate to patients far better than many of his colleagues.

He continues. "I have reviewed all of your

73

tests and can tell you your condition is quite serious. But the fact that you are still alive means there is always hope, and I would like to tell you what I believe is the best course of action for us to take."

I like this doctor more with each passing minute. He exudes confidence and hope even in my obviously dire condition. For the next hour he talks about the various medicines he can use and their various side effect. He answers the myriad of questions my wife has, and I can see her confidence is also growing in this doctor. He also reviews the frequency of scans he will be doing to confirm what is happening with the aneurism.

"As Dr. Baine told you, you need to be prepared for the worst, but as long as the vein has not ruptured, there is still hope that we can reduce the pressure on it, and maybe lessen the chance it will rupture." His final words again fill me with a sense of hope that perhaps I was being spared not only to perform the tasks at hand, but that perhaps I would have more time with my wife and my daughter.

But what happens next shocks and pleases me even more.

"You folks are Christians?"

"Yes, we are," Carol responds, answering before I could.

He nods, saying, "I am too. I thought you might be when I heard you praying when I opened the door. If you don't mind, I would like to pray with you as well, as I believe only the Lord permits my skills and knowledge to actually make a difference."

For the next ten minutes he joins us, and I hear his pleading for guidance, to make a difference with the condition I have and the uncertain immediate future I am facing. I immediately understand why this man exudes hope, because his confidence comes not from his abilities, but from the One he follows who holds everything in His hands and under His control.

74

When we are done praying and he stands and prepares to depart, it is Laura who asks a question that stops him.

"What about Jonathan? Can anything be done for him?"

Dr. Charles slowly sits down again. He is considering what he can or should share. But he finally reaches a decision and says, "Jonathan has a very rare and very aggressive cancer. Jonathan's father is the most skilled physician I have ever met or worked with. Frankly, in the human sense, Jonathan could not have a better physician than his own father. But this cancer is not one that we as doctors have much success with. Frankly, it will take a miracle to save that young boy. I do not understand at times why the Lord allows these things to happen to such young people, or for that matter to anyone. But I also know He is always at work, even in these terrible situations, and somehow what is occurring will still fulfill a purpose that He has for this.

"I believe in miracles, and from the first day I heard of what Jonathan is facing, I have been praying for one. That is what it is going to take, and I do not know whether the Lord is going to provide a miracle for Jonathan. And I am praying for his father as well. He is in a terrible place. He is the best there is in this world as far as medical skill and it's not enough. He is at a loss as to what to do, and he has nowhere to turn. I've tried talking to him, but there is a wall up that I haven't been able to penetrate. I think I've damaged our friendship by trying to push too hard, and now I am praying for a miracle for him as well."

His last words are spoken with a well of emotion. Again, I am already silently thanking the Lord for Dr. Charles.

"Sorry, I wish I had better news to give you, Laura." He addresses my daughter by name for the first time.

75

"Yes, we will be praying for a miracle for Jonathan as well," Laura responds, and I see her eyes flash intensity of purpose. Dr. Charles sees her eyes as well, and I watch his smile return. "I am sure you will, and as you know, prayers are never not answered, even if we do not get the answer we may be wanting."

After the doctor leaves, Carol, Laura, and I talk a little further and then the nurse arrives with my dinner. She smiles at my wife and daughter as she sits my bed up and slides the tray table my way. "You know, our cafeteria is still open, and this might be a good time for you to also get some food," she offers.

They agree, and after they are gone, I say a prayer again, giving thanks for the food, for Dr. Charles, and for my life, and I pray for the miracle both Jonathan and I need and ask that if a miracle is not His will, that He give us both the strength to run the race left before us. I then remember Jonathan's father, and I add that prayer for that miracle as well.

Chapter Nine – The Love Of A Mother

My wife and daughter return to my room after a two-hour break. I know they must have gone home, as both are dressed in fresh clothes, and both appear to have showered as well. I know something is wrong as soon as I see my daughter's countenance. Her face reflects a mix of sadness, frustration, and anger. My wife is subdued as well but her facial expression does not reveal her actual frame of mind as my daughter's does.

I start the conversation asking, "What's wrong?"

My wife responds, cutting off the outburst I expect from my daughter.

"Jonathan has been moved out of the hospital. We stopped by the nurse's station on the way here, asking for Jonathan's room number, and they informed us that Jonathan is no longer in the hospital. They would not tell us where he has been moved to, only that he is no longer here."

Before I can respond to that news, the door to my room opens again, and my friend, The Stork, is once again looking in at us, and his face has a sad smile.

"I see you've heard Jonathan has moved from the hospital," Louis says.

I simply nod and Louis continues,

"Jonathan's father has moved him back home, and he has taken some time off to care for his son at home. Based on what I have been able to learn, they are not expecting Jonathan to last much more than a month, if even that, and both Jonathan's father and mother did not want him to die here. There is really nothing more they can do for him medically other than trying to keep him comfortable while the cancer runs its course."

"I understand why they would want to take him

home," I respond.

As a father, I really do understand the difficult position Jonathan's father is in, and I actually agree with the decision to take him home. And despite our differences, I am glad his father has taken time off from his work to be with his son. I didn't believe he would leave his position here, but I am glad he made that decision.

I look over at my daughter, and her facial expression has changed to one of just sadness. "It's not fair." Her words spoken softly, she looks immensely tired, as if the news Jonathan has left the hospital has uncorked her bottle of energy, and suddenly the last week has finally caught up with her.

"Dad, I really don't feel like reading any more this evening. Would it be okay if I just go back home? I think I need to sleep." Her words again reflect a tiredness uncommon for her. I look at my wife, and see her nod, signaling me of her acceptance of that request.

"Sure, Laura, that is fine. We can pick up the story tomorrow if that is okay with you." My words seem to resolve some of the struggle my daughter is engaged in, and she steps over to my bed and gives me a hug before she starts for the door. My wife quickly does the same, and says, "We will see you in the morning, Rubin." And then they are gone.

After the door closes, Louis sits down in the chair Carol normally sits in, and I find the raise button and lift my head until I am level with Louis's gaze. "You going to share the rest of the story?" I ask. Louis shakes his head and begins.

"I think I lost a friend today," he opens with. "When Jeremey made it back to Jonathan's room, he asked to speak with me outside the room. Let's just say, I got a tongue lashing the likes of which I don't believe I have ever had before, except maybe when I was a young lad and broke my father's favorite fishing

78

pole! Anyway, when it was over, I tried to explain why I had brought Jonathan here, but he was still so angry I gave up.

"I was downstairs speaking with some friends when I saw Jonathan's mother arrive, and then two nurses and Jeremey brought Jonathan down in a wheelchair, and I watched as they left the hospital together. I think Jonathan saw me, but he looked scared and lost, and I did not realize just how small he really has become until then. He always appeared bigger to me. There was something in his banter that just made him seem so much larger and vibrant than he really is." Louis falls silent, his thoughts obviously dwelling on that departing image of Jonathan.

"You've been a good friend to Jonathan, and I suspect Jeremey will come to see that soon as well."

My words seem to bring some relief to my friend. He nods and then stands. "You know, you and I have been around for a long time. We've had our spats, but always have managed to talk things though. I think you are now my oldest and longest-living friend. I'm not too sure I will get to mend my friendship with Jeremey."

"I think I need to rest as well, old friend. I will be back in the morning, as I want to hear more of the story, so tell Laura to wait until I get here."

He opens the door, and I say, "Goodnight, Louis, and thanks." He nods again and then is gone.

My friendship with Louis is now more than 70 years long. We met in school and have literally gone through more events together than most married people experience. Seeing him so despondent after the confrontation with Jonathan's father drives me back to thinking about and praying for Jeremey and for Jonathan. My eyes close, and the next thing I know, a nurse is poking me and asking if I'm awake. It's three in the morning—hospitals. Of course I wasn't awake, but I am now. I almost say something, but then

79

remember how grateful I am to still be here.

After that poke and prod routine, I do fall back to sleep but only after I again talk with the Lord and pray for my wife and daughter. I am still not sure I know why He has kept me here, but I am grateful for every minute He gives me with Carol and Laura, and I make sure to tell him that.

I am awake when the same nurse arrives back in my room a little after six in the morning. This time I smile at her and say, "Good morning." She smiles back, and I realize she looks really tired. "You pull the all-night shift often?" I ask her.

She just smiles and says, "Actually, it was a double shift. Several of the nurses are sick, and they asked me to stay on. I normally head home at 6:30 p.m., but today it will be in about a half hour." She has with her a small cup that holds several pills, and another cup with the traditional red hospital straw and what I assume is water.

"These are your new medicines Dr. Browning ordered for you. It may make you a bit groggy, so it is fine to fall back to sleep if you like."

I take the four pills, each a different shape and color. The fluid is water, and it is cold. For whatever reason, I like water best when it is really cold, preferable with ice in it, or steaming hot with sugar, cream and coffee. There is no in-between for me. I look at her badge that has her name on it and see Maggie Malone under her picture.

"Thank you, Maggie."

She smiles at me, and says, "Mr. James, I am glad you made it back to us. I really like your wife, and your daughter is," she hesitates for a moment and then completes the thought, "interesting."

I've heard Laura called many things. Many people are put off by the purple hair color and the dozen piercings marking her ears, nose, and tongue. And her eyes, well they can be a bit frightening at

80

times. But "interesting" is a new one for me.

"Interesting?" I ask.

Maggie stops for a moment and then explains her observation. "Yes, when I first saw her, I was put off by, well, the way she looks, but then I heard her talking with Mrs. Baine and her son Jonathan this morning, and she speaks with such conviction and authority. It's like the way she looks is a disguise that hides an incredible bright and passionate person."

"This morning?" I ask, confirming again that the digital clock is saying 6:10 a.m. now.

"Yes, they've been here since a little after 4 a.m., just sitting in the waiting room talking," she responds.

"Is my wife with them as well?" I ask.

"She is now, but she got here just before six. They asked me if you were awake, and I told them I would go check, that I needed to," once again she pauses, thinking, " 'poke and prod' you, I think your daughter called it. Anyway, I will let them know you are awake, but I will warn them the new medicine may make you sleepy in a bit."

Maggie leaves, and when the door reopens, it is not my wife, or my daughter, but my friend, The Stork, who arrives first.

"It's six-thirty in the morning. What are you doing here?" I ask Louis.

He smiles, and then responds, "Yes, I know it is early, that is what I told Laura when she called me. But then she told me that Jonathan and Katherine were here, and that she wanted to begin reading the story again as soon as possible. So, I got here as fast as I could, because I didn't want to miss anything, and I wanted to see Jonathan again."

The door opens again, and my wife holds the door while a tall, well-dressed and incredibly attractive woman pushes the wheelchair in which Jonathan sits. I immediately see the similarities

81

between mother and son. While Jonathan has his father's eyes, his face shape, his thin fine nose and lips are similar to the woman who is now in front of me. My daughter follows them in, carrying her bundle of papers with her, and it's Jonathan who announces their arrival.

"Hi, Mr. Rubin. I'm glad you are finally awake!" His voice is stronger than it was before, but Louis is right, in that wheelchair he looks incredibly small for being a ten-year-old boy. But he looks neither frightened nor lost. Instead his eyes are bright, and he beams with an intensity that seems to deny the illness that is eating away at him. It is his mother who steps into the conversation.

"Mr. James."

"Rubin," I say, interrupting her opening.

"Okay, Rubin, I'm sorry we are disturbing you so early. My name is Katherine Baine, and I am Jonathan's mom. Jonathan has been talking about you non-stop since he got home, and he asked me to take him back to the hospital, so he could hear more of the story your daughter is telling you."

"At four in the morning?" I interrupt her again, sharing that piece of news I had gleaned from Maggie.

"Yes, we got here pretty early. Jonathan could not sleep, and well, neither could I. He showed me this." She removes from her purse the small pouch with the long necklace-like piece of cloth and then removes the gold coin from the pouch. She studies it for only a moment, and then slides the coin back into the pouch, and hands it to her son. Jonathan quietly takes it and slips it around his neck and allows the pouch to slide down under the T-shirt he is wearing.

"For me, that coin is an amazing find. You see, my hobby is collecting coins from all over the world. Jonathan could tell you that I am a well-known numismatist, and when he showed me the coin, I was amazed at its condition. I knew what it was, because I

82

have this." Reaching back into her purse she extracts a small box and opens it, revealing a similar-looking coin. While the coin looks similar, it is so worn only the image of the emperor ties the two coins together as being the same. "But what really intrigued me was the story Jonathan told me about where the coin came from, and how he came into possession of it." She stops for a moment, letting all of what she has said sink in. "Would it be okay if we stay to listen to the story Laura is reading?" It is then I realize she has her overcoat still on.

"Sure, take your coat off and perhaps you can sit with Laura on that chair." I point to the bench-like chair that has been Laura's place for much of the time she has been here.

Louis does the math quickly and says, "I'll be right back." Katherine pushes Jonathan's wheelchair over to the bench and takes her coat off, draping it over the back side of the chair. She is wearing a stylish set of jeans and a colorful shirt that perfectly outlines her athletic frame. There is no question, she really is a beautiful woman.

I look at Katherine and feel I must tell her of the discussion with Jeremey, before we begin the story again. "Mrs. Baine—"

"Katherine," she says, interrupting me and setting the same rule I had when she first arrived. She has now sat down on the edge of the chair next to her son's wheelchair, leaving more than two thirds of the seat for Laura.

I smile at the obvious similarity and continue. "Katherine, I need to tell you that your husband explicitly asked that I not speak with your son any further. While I didn't agree with his request, I need you to understand what he said and be sure you can explain why you brought Jonathan back here."

Katherine looks thoughtfully at me. "Rubin, Jeremey means well. He has done everything he

83

knows to do for Jonathan. He also knows that I am a Christian. My father warned me of the potential conflict we would have in our marriage if I went ahead and married him, with him not believing what I believe. I didn't listen to my father, because I was and still am so in love with Jeremey. He is a good man. He loves me and he loves our son. But my belief does cause issues for us. I've mostly gone along with what my husband has wanted.

"Frankly, I haven't been going to church much, and I have allowed my son to grow up without many of the stories my dad and mom shared with me when I was a young girl. But when Jonathan got sick, and everything that Jeremey was trying was not working, I knew the only place I could go was back to God. I've been asking him to forgive me, and to save our son. I started reading the Bible stories to Jonathan. Jeremey and I had one of our very rare fights over that. I stopped reading the stories to Jonathan, but where I failed, God has made a different path.

"Before we decided to bring Jonathan home, we had quite a discussion about who was going to set the rules for Jonathan's care once he came home. Jeremey agreed that I would be the one making the decisions on his care once he came home. Jeremey knows I'm here. I promised him he would always know what I was doing, and why. He knows I'm here, because you and your family have given something to Jonathan neither I nor my husband have been able to give. You've given him hope." She says those last words, even as she lays her hand lightly on her son's shoulder. "I'm here to understand what it is that has so changed him."

The door to my room opens again, and Louis is carrying a chair into the room, and surprisingly, I see Maggie right behind him carrying another chair. I think Maggie sees my questioning look, and before I can ask, she answers, "I heard Jonathan talking about

84

the story that brought him and his mom back to the hospital, and then I heard your daughter reading that story from the Bible and talking about it, and hearing her say it was Lazarus's story. I decided I wanted to hear the story as well, and I am off work now." I just smile and realize somewhere in that statement was the request for permission, and then as if she has read that thought as well, she asks, "Of course, if that is okay with you?"

"Of course, you are welcome to stay."

While Maggie is introducing herself to my wife and to Katherine and Jonathan, I am looking over at my daughter. She knows the question I am going to ask. It is like everyone can read my mind this morning. I never get to ask, *"Why did you come back here at four in the morning, and how did you get here?"*

She speaks softly, to the point that the other conversations in the room drown out her words, except for my ears. "He told me to come here, and I am eighteen, Dad, and I have a car."

I know who "He" is. Like I said, she is much better at listening than I am. I can see in her eyes that she doesn't want to talk more about what drove her to come back and that at some point she will tell me the rest of the story.

Laura waits until all the introductions are done, and everyone is now seated and looking at her. She has already found the spot where she left off from the story, and she begins reading.

85

Chapter Ten – Abounding Miracles

"What would you expect if God were walking in your midst?"

I have often thought about that question, and often when I am talking with people who know my story, I ask that question. I knew Jesus as a carpenter's son, as a gifted carpenter, as a friend, and as the single-most prolific miracle worker ever to walk this earth. The next question I would ask those questioning me would be "How difficult do you believe it was for me to come to belief that this friend was actually the Creator shrouded in our likeness, walking among us, and calling me His friend?" Remember, I had known him since we were children. I saw him as a person like myself, who loved to play and talk. I saw Joseph teach him his trade, and I touched the table he had made almost daily for much of my young life.

Our scriptures predict a time when one would come who would drive demons out, heal many kinds of sickness, and claim the throne of David as his own. Even David, the greatest of our kings, would pen of his future lineage, that this One would be greater than he was because He existed before him. How was that possible? To exist before David, our king, and yet be born long after David died? That Psalm has often echoed in my mind, when I consider what happened in the three years between the arrival of John the Baptist and that terrible day when Jesus's life was taken, and what followed afterward.

I could speak of many of the miracles he worked, but others have already done that, so I will tell the story of the four that have touched me so personally. It has always amazed me that providence would put so many people and the events that involved them in our small village. Bethany would be the focus of many of the most significant miracles, and many of the people to experience those miracles firsthand would live there.

The first of these is the story of a man who was of even greater means than my parents, but who was struck down with the dreaded scourge of leprosy.

In our culture and in our religion, there is almost no affliction more detestable than this one. A person who is stricken with leprosy is usually driven outside the village, and when that person is in the vicinity of others, they must cry out: "Unclean, Unclean," to alert those other people of their condition. To have flesh rotting away on your own body is one of the most awful experiences any person can have, and to become a social outcast from your friends, family, and neighbors, an even a greater sorrow.

Jesus not only would heal lepers, but he would physically touch many of them, making himself exposed to both that uncleanness but also to the potential of the disease itself. Simon of Bethany was one such individual. His name is inseparably attached with the affliction he at one time bore.

One thing about coming from such a small place like Bethany. Everyone knew everybody who lived there. There were very few secrets that could be kept hidden. And when a person has wealth, who they are is of even more interest.

Simon was not born with leprosy. He contracted the condition only after he had built a trading business that had made him one of the wealthiest men in Bethany, and in fact in all our country. Because of his wealth, he was able to hide himself away from most people after he caught the disease. He seldom ventured outside, instead using his means to have food and other necessities brought to him. He managed to live for many years in our village, but because of his great care, he was never driven out, but his condition was known by many, and his wealth protected him.

Simon learned Jesus was healing many and heard where he was ministering. Simon left Bethany in the middle of the night, making sure no one saw his exit. He

88

walked several days, always avoiding other travelers, until he found Jesus. When he saw Jesus, he removed his coverings, exposing to all who were following Jesus the full extent of his affliction. He told me of the reaction of the people who quickly withdrew from his vicinity when they saw his body had been ravaged by the disease.

If there had been more time, many of the people would likely have picked up stones to throw at him to drive him away. But he took those few seconds to approach Jesus where he bowed down before him and said, "Lord, if you are willing, you can make me clean."

What happened next would change Simon's life forever and would cause Simon to become a follower and friend of Jesus as well. Jesus reached out and touched Simon, handling his flesh that was rotting away, saying, "I am willing, be cleansed." The instant Jesus touched Simon, his flesh began healing. Those five words changed everything. Jesus was willing to touch Simon, to understand the great scourge that defined Simon's life. He willed Simon's flesh to be freed from the disease, and in an instant that disease fled, and what it had consumed became whole. Jesus was willing to touch what others were too afraid to even see.

Simon would often be asked, "what did he do," or "what did it feel like?" Simon would only repeat, "He touched me, and the leprosy was gone and where rot existed now firm flesh was found." Jesus told him to go to the priests and to offer the sacrifice of thanksgiving required for the healing. Our scriptures direct how a person stricken with leprosy and then healed was to show themself to the priest so they could confirm the person was free of the disease. Simon did them both in the village where he was healed, and upon his return to Bethany. His story only added to the fame and excitement about the miracle worker from Nazareth.

When Simon returned to Bethany after he went to the priests and was declared clean, he went to all those who had helped him for so many years, finally able to

89

thank them in person for their ministry to him, even though he had paid everyone well for their services. I and my sisters had provided many ointments and salves to Simon, and it would be my sister Mary who would introduce Simon to one of Cain's sisters, who would later become his wife. Martha also had prepared food for Simon during those years, and Simon would call upon her gifts often when he would host people now in his home. His home had even a larger eating and serving area than ours and was very close to our own home. That fact would play a significant role in a future event that would shape me and my sisters and would become how my family is remembered now.

As I said, when you live in such a small village, nothing remains a secret for very long. The healing of Simon became known to the others who had various afflictions including Cain, who had been blind from birth. Cain's story, and his miracle would be the second-greatest miracle to occur within our little village, but that would happen much later in Jesus's ministry and only shortly before I would experience the true identity of the carpenter's son.

Cain was the fifth child of Samuel the Potter and Lydia. His sightless condition was immediately known, as where orbs normally were found, only hollowed-out depressions existed. The condition caused his face to appear unfinished. Yet, the rest of his body was untouched. He certainly had a good set of lungs as his parents would attest to shortly after his birth. But his sightless condition marked him as flawed.

My first real interaction with Cain would not occur until he was approaching ten years old. His father took their entire family to the temple the same year that Jesus became of age, during the Passover festival. Because of Cain's condition, he was considered damaged, and the temple guards were not going to let him in. Jesus found Cain there and using his already considerable understanding of the law, asked the guards: *"Does the law require wholeness of body or wholeness of spirit?"*

Jesus brought Cain into the temple, and a dream Cain had nurtured his entire young life was fulfilled. He sat where Samuel the prophet had sat, and whispered those same words, "Lord speak, your servant is listening." While no voice had answered his prayer, his heart still exalted in merely being in the temple.

Jesus found me in the temple and asked that I take Cain back home. That was my first real interaction with the young blind boy. I asked Cain during our walk home, "How long have you known Jesus?" His response surprised me.

"Thank you, I did not know his name. This was the first time I met him. He found me crying and took me to the temple. They were not going to let me in, but he spoke a single question to them, and they let me pass."

"Why were you crying?" I asked. The whole terrible experience of his morning came tumbling out, his accidental collision with the stack of the pots his father had been making for the order my father had placed. The crescendo of breaking pottery and his father's angry outburst.

After I returned Cain to his home, I returned to mine. I explained to my father what had happened to Cain in his father's workshop. My father had listened quietly and then said, "Thank you for being a friend to Cain. I will talk with Samuel, and I think we can remedy the problem."

Later I learned my father had extended the contract with Cain's father and doubled his order at a higher price, to ensure no loss would occur from Cain's accident. I also learned that Cain had used the gold coin my father had given him during his earlier confrontation with the ruffians who had attacked the beggars, to try to pay his father for the damage he had caused. Cain had not told the full story of how he had come by that coin, making it sound like it had been earned through

91

begging. That event set in motion the decisions that would result in Cain taking up a place with the other beggars in Bethany at the small ledge that lined the path heading from Bethany to the great city.

For close to twenty years, Cain would rise every day and take his place among the beggars at that location. I would often stop and talk with him, and I discovered that despite his blindness, he had a quick wit, and a friendly attitude. But he also had those days when a black mood would fall over him as he considered his condition and his lot in life.

My parents' death was the second time I had a meaningful discussion with Cain. When I met him, Cain's heart was once again laid bare to me. His words still pierce my heart when I consider the deep well they flooded up from. We spoke for a long time, but I will relay only a small portion, as much of the back and forth was two men, two friends, two mourners, coming to terms with the loss we had both experienced.

"I loved your father. He is one of the only people who ever cared for me. His kindness to me was greater than any of my family members. He saw me as a person, not as something less. There have been very few who look upon me without pity and consider my life as valuable. I do not understand how God would allow his life to be taken in such a way."

That final sentence was said in a tone of deep hurt and anger. I knew he was wrestling with God himself. I understood the emotion, for I had spent much of the last two days in the same condition. When I left him, he was still in a bad place.

I had not given him the coin and the pouch back as our discussion had opened no doors for that to happen. His whole attitude changed, and for more than a year he would no longer be the friendly beggar he had been up to that time. His meager collection became even smaller, as he no longer was able to ask for those gifts that would provide for his needs. Surly and rude

92

beggars do not endear themselves to those needing to be encouraged to part with their charity. He also stopped much of the basic hygiene that kept odors away, and soon he literally smelled a little like death itself.

It would be almost a year before two events occurred that would snap him out of his anger. The first was meeting Simon the Leper, who shared with him his own story and his faith in God despite his affliction. The second occurred later that same evening, and he would tell of a visit from the same person who had taken him to the temple the first time. Cain was not sure whether it was a dream or something that had really happened. All he remembered was that Jesus had returned him to the temple in the middle of the night and had admonished him for his anger. "The father makes no mistakes, and only the father has the right to the anger you now harbor." Jesus had gone further, telling Cain of the origin of his name, of the anger that resulted in the first murder, and of the danger remaining in this frame of mind would put him in.

When he awoke in the morning, he was in the stable he often used as his sleeping place, and he was uncertain how he had arrived there. Jesus had also pressed the coin and pouch back into his hand, reminding him that Joseph had given him an emblem of hope, not one of despair. That dream or visit, broke Cain's anger. The presence of the pouch and coin convinced him it was more than a dream. How else would he have received them back?

The next morning when Mary found him, he was in a clear mind and no longer angry. He left her quickly to bathe and remove the clothes that had been on him for more than a year. His coin and pouch, well that I had returned to the grave of my parents shortly after my aborted attempt at returning them to Cain. I had kept it for a while, hidden away in our home, but finally decided I had no good way to explain to Cain why he should take it back. It would be more than another year

93

before Jesus visited our home again. I never did inquire about that event, and how Jesus had found the coin and pouch, or why he had not visited with us if he was visiting with Cain.

Fortunately, Cain returned to being the normally cheerful, always-thoughtful person he had been earlier. The next ten years passed by quickly, and Cain had just entered his thirtieth year, and Jesus was more than two years into his ministry when everything would change for Cain.

Jesus was heading toward Jerusalem again. Already a host of people had been healed. Simon the Leper, Jacob the paralytic, even Ruth, my future wife, and her friend Caleb had experienced the power of Jesus's ministry. It had been reported that twice he had fed the massive crowds of people following him when practically no food had been available. News about this prophet/healer from Nazareth was echoing across our land. As Jesus entered Bethany, it was clear he would not stop by our home as he made his way toward Jerusalem, but he would pass by the perch where Cain and the other beggars sat.

I was not there to see the interaction between Jesus and Cain. Martha, though, was in the crowd following Jesus. She heard the question one of Jesus's disciples asked.

"Rabbi, who sinned, this man or his parents, that he would be born blind?"

Later, Cain would confirm that this question had echoed in his own soul for most of his life. What had his parents done that would have caused such a great malady to be manifested in their son? For much of his life, he had assumed it had to be something they had done, for what could he have possibly done before birth to deserve such punishment?

But Jesus's answer would shatter all those assumptions. "It was neither that this man sinned, nor his parents, but it was so that the works of God might be

94

displayed in him. We must work the works of Him who sent Me, as long as it is day; night is coming when no one can work, While I am in the world, I am the Light of the world."

Cain shared with me his surprise at those words. He had been born blind, created that way, for this very moment. For thirty years he had suffered with the condition; his parents had lived with the shame and burden of an infirmed son, and it had been the deliberate purpose of God, so that what was about to happen, could. What work was Jesus talking about? What did it mean the night was coming, or that he was the light of the world?

Jesus had bent down to the ground, spat on the dust, and made a clay of the spittle and dirt and then applied that clay to his Cain's eyes. He told Cain, "Go wash in the pool of Siloam."

Jesus left Cain there, and the crowds of people passed him by. Cain felt the warm clay on his face, and on his own he made the half mile walk to the pool Jesus had mentioned. He washed his face in the pool, felt the clay take on new form, and saw the water dripping through his hands and into the pool. For the first time in his life, he saw his face, and he had eyes. Light flooded Cain's mind, and his bright green eyes flashed with the lightening. Tears flowed freely from these new-formed eyes as Cain wept for joy.

Cain made it back to his perch. It had taken him longer than he had expected. He was unsure of the way, having always felt his way there before, but now seeing, everything was different, strange. He had to close his eyes several times, to get his bearings. The first few times he feared this new sight would disappear, but each time when he reopened his eyes, sight was still there. His arrival back into the village caused an incredible stir. People who had seen him daily for years did not recognize him. His face was so completely changed people would say, "No, but he is like him." He had to

95

convince people who had known him his whole life, that in fact, it was the same person who had before lacked eyes, who stood before them.

The commotion became so great, the neighbors took him to the Pharisees, who were the spiritual leaders in Bethany, to get the answers everyone wanted. "How is it, that you, having been born blind, now see?"

That question was asked so many times, in so many different ways, but Cain's answer was always the same. "He put clay on my face, and I washed, and now I see." Now the day of the miracle was a Sabbath, and some of the Pharisees exclaimed that Jesus had sinned for making the clay was work, and on the Sabbath no work was to be done. But the arguments just continued to flow. How could such a miracle occur on the Sabbath if the means used in the miracle involved work? One potential answer was that no miracle had occurred at all and that the man before them was not Cain, the blind beggar, but someone else.

They called Cain's parents to come and verify that this person before them was in fact their son who had been born blind. They asked his parents, "Is this your son, who you say was born blind? Then how does he now see?" His parents already knew anyone who pointed to Jesus and claimed he was the Christ was to be put out of the synagogue and affirming that Jesus had performed this miracle was tantamount to that confession.

His parents did answer but kicked the final question back to Cain. "We know that this is our son and that he was born blind, but how he now sees, we do not know, or who opened his eyes, we do not know. Ask him, he is of age; he will speak for himself."

The Pharisees brought Cain back in, and said, "Give glory to God, we know that this man is a sinner."

Cain answered, "Whether he is a sinner, I do not know; one thing I do know though I was blind now I see."

96

The protests continued, and again they asked the same question, saying, "What did He do to you? How did He open your eyes?"

Cain was almost at a loss for words. He had told them so many times, but they would not accept what he was saying. "I told you already, and you did not listen; why do you want to hear it again? You do not want to become his disciples too, do you?" It was at that moment something had solidified in Cain's thinking. He knew whatever their answer, he did want to be a disciple of Jesus.

Their response was to revile Cain and claim he was already a disciple of Jesus, but they were disciples of Moses. Certainly, they thought, Moses is more important than this man.

To drive that point home, they said, "We know that God has spoken to Moses, but as for this man, we do not know where he is from."

Cain was stunned by their answer and from deep in his soul a thought turned into a conviction. They were lying. It was evident where this man had come from. And at that same instant Cain felt a stirring in his mind that soon became a fire burning within his soul. Those in the room saw the flashes of fire flickering in his newly seeing eyes. Cain looked around the room, his eyes taking in the judges of Bethany and then spoke.

"Well, here is an amazing thing that you do not know where He is from, and yet he opened my eyes. We know that God does not hear sinners but if anyone is God fearing and does His will, He hears him. Since the beginning of time it has never been heard that anyone opened the eyes of a person born blind. If this man were not from God, He could do nothing."

Cain's statement enraged the Pharisees, and they reverted to the belief that it was because of Cain's sin, that he was born blind. They rejected the very statement that Jesus had made, which cleared out of Cain's mind forever the thought that his condition was because of sin

97

in either his parents' or his own life. Cain's assertion had called their refusal to acknowledge what was evident—the lie that it was. Their judgement was to cast Cain out of the Synagogue

"You were born, entirely in sins, and are you teaching us?"

Now, being cast out of the synagogue was a terrible price to pay. It meant you were no longer welcomed among the believers and could no longer be in the place where the scriptures were read and explained. It was for that reason both Samuel and Lydia had turned the final question back to their son. But for Cain, the line had been crossed, but not by him. They had lied to themselves. What Jesus had done testified clearly of where he had come from. Only a prophet from God could possibly be doing these things, and no prophet before had ever given eyes to one born without them. This man was something even greater, and Cain would quickly discover just who Jesus really was.

Shortly after Cain had been put out of the Synagogue, Jesus found him. Cain did not recognize him, but when Jesus spoke, his voice identified him for Cain. Cain looked for the first time upon the man who had taken him to the temple twice now, and who had given him sight. Jesus's words to him though were not the ones anyone would have expected. Looking into Cain's eyes, Jesus said, "Do you believe in the Son of Man?"

"The Son of Man." Cain understood the question. Jesus was asking him if he believed in the Messiah, the one who was to come and rescue all of Israel. Cain explained the effect that question had on him. "I felt every nerve in my body tingling, and his words pierced my heart. I knew this man had given me my sight and had shown compassion toward me when others sought to exclude me, and he had snapped my anger when I was lost in my grief. I had not put all the pieces together yet, so I asked Jesus, 'Who is he Lord, that I may believe in

98

him?' I knew who ever this man pointed to must surely be that person."

His answer brought all the pieces together. "You have both seen Him, and He is the one who is talking with you."

Cain stared at Jesus only momentarily, before knelling in front of him saying: "Lord, I believe."

That confession brought another confrontation with the Pharisees who were also following Jesus and seeking any opportunity to discredit him. After that confrontation, their plotting to kill Jesus would enter a much more serious level of planning. Jesus was aware of their plans and withdrew from the area of Bethany and of Jerusalem, heading back to the area where John the Baptist and he had first met, where John had been baptizing people. He would remain there until another person who had a need even greater than Cain's would result in the most significant miracle of his ministry. That miracle would solidify the urgency of the need to kill Jesus and anyone who pointed to the uniqueness of his ministry. That would lead directly to the reason I have lived on this island so far away from my home.

Often, people, when talking of my life and my particular role in confirming who Jesus is, would forget that mine was not the only story of the most miraculous events in his ministry. Both Ruth, who became my wife, and her friend Caleb had been touched by Jesus in ways like my own story. I will tell you their stories first before I will tell you the rest of mine. I have found that the magnitude of the number of miracles performed by Jesus, and the number of lives changed by his presence is often a part in drawing people to understanding who Jesus is.

Laura has been reading for a little more than two hours. When she stops, I see instantly the amount of energy she has spent in the reading of the story. What most people do not know is she is not merely reading the words penned here. In fact, within her mind, the original

99

text in Aramaic is still present, and she is reconfirming every word in her translation even as she reads what Carol had transcribed originally. It is part of the gift that has a great cost. My daughter's mind has created a photograph of what she has translated, and when she reads the words on the paper, she is also looking at the image, like a teleprompter, where she is confirming again the accuracy of her version.

I see her face and say, "Let's take a break for a moment and get some food, and I need to use the bathroom as well." As if on cue, the door opens and another nurse enters and stops, taking in the crowd of six people in the room. It's time for my "poking and prodding." The hospital has a rule that only two people are supposed to visit at any one time. I see the surprise on the new nurse's face but she sees Maggie, who nods and stands, heading over to the new nurse.

"Hi, Sue." Taking her colleague by her elbow, they walk back outside to talk. Everyone else is now standing, except Laura, who has closed her eyes and seems to be shaking off the weariness of the past two hours.

I really do need to use the bathroom, and Louis seeing my discomfort says, "Let's give Rubin a few minutes." Even Laura stands and walks with Louis, Carol, and Katherine, pushing Jonathan to the door. Once they have left and the door has closed, I reach for that silver pan that serves its purpose.

If you have never had to use one of these "bedpans" consider yourself fortunate. Trying to position it without making a mess is practically impossible by oneself. But just as I am about to give up, Sue returns alone. She immediately understands my predicament and aids me in positioning the pan. When I have finished, she also helps me wipe myself and then changes my robe. Like I say, count your blessings if you have never had to use one of these things. Let's just say, there is no modesty to be had when you need to go, and

100

you cannot walk yourself to the bathroom.

"Let's get you up," Sue says and then helps me wrestle out of the bed and into the chair Carol is normally sitting in. It's then I see the stained sheet and understand what Sue is doing. Ah, yes…bedpans.

After Sue has changed the dirty linen and before she helps me back into the bed, she takes my blood pressure, temperature, and makes sure the IV and other wires are still fastened to my body correctly. She walks over to the computer positioned close to my bed and is making the notes of her visit. She reads something on the computer, and then finds the needle and the vials in one of the drawers. Like I said, this is part of the "poke."

After she has taken the required sample of blood, she smiles and says, "Your breakfast will be here shortly," and then leaves. The clock says 8:30 a.m. Sue has been remarkably silent about where the crowd of visitors is and whether they will be allowed to return. My breakfast arrives, an interesting combination of juice, eggs, toast, and something that passes as sausage. There is also the requisite white cup with the red straw. I reach for the water first. Still, no visitors.

Chapter Eleven – Lots of Questions, Few Answers

When the door finally opens more than an hour later it's Katherine pushing Jonathan. Jonathan smiles, calling out, "Hi, Mr. Rubin, we're back."

What I wasn't expecting is the third person who walks in behind them. Dr. Jeremey Baine, Jonathan's father, is here as well. He does not look happy to be here, but he smiles a crooked smile when he realizes I have seen him. He breaks the awkward silence.

"Mr. James."

"Rubin," I interject, once again interrupting him.

"Okay, Rubin. My wife and son called me and asked me to come to talk with you. I'm here only because of them. As you already know, I don't believe the fairy tales you are all talking about, and I believe it is a waste of whatever time we have left together."

His words and tone have a sense of futility and sadness laced throughout. It is also at that moment, that I see he is holding in one of his hands the small pouch with the coin enclosed. Jonathan has given that emblem of hope to his father. Jonathan must realize I see the pouch. I turn to Jonathan, and I understand instantly what Jonathan's face is communicating. He doesn't say anything, but I see in his bright eyes the reason. At the very least Jonathan doesn't want his condition to be the cause of such sadness in his father, and he understands that hopelessness is at the root of that sadness. Jonathan gave him that emblem of hope because his father needs it ever more than himself.

I can imagine how difficult it is for Jonathan to be facing what he is, only to have that burden increased by his father's own despair over the situation. Jonathan does not wait for me to say anything, instead he starts.

"Mr. Rubin, in the story, the blindman learns that neither he nor his parents are to blame for his condition. I'm not sure I understand how he thought either he or his parents are to be blamed. Can you explain that to me?"

103

Leave it to a child to pick one of the questions at the core of the story.

I looked around and realize that Laura has taken the translation with her but sitting on the bench seat next to Kathryn is her "Source" book. I look at Kathryn and ask her, "Kathryn, would you mind taking my daughter's Bible and reading John chapter 9 for us?" I look at Jeremey, but he isn't about to object, and Kathryn has already retrieved the book and is flipping through the pages. "It starts on page 914 in her Bible," I add, allowing Kathryn to find the location faster. Kathryn begins reading the account, and about ten minutes later finishes as she reads the last verse in the chapter.

I look at Jonathan and now tackle the question he has asked, already suspecting what his follow-up question will be. I review the common thought that our condition in this life is solely based on what we have done. "You can see that those with Jesus, who were His followers, assumed it was something either the parents or the man had done, which was the reason for his condition. But Jesus sort of rips up that notion and instead places before them another reason, that God had created the blind man that way, in order that the miracle that Jesus was about to perform would be set up to occur. If the man had not been born blind, the significance of the miracle would have been lessened."

Jeremey's head is already shaking, and he finally speaks.

"So, you are telling us that a 'good' God has willingly allowed this man to be born without eyes, to not only force this man to suffer his entire life with that infirmity, but to put the man's parents and family through all of the struggle and humiliation of having a child with such a condition, only to cue up a miracle?"

I don't miss the sarcasm in his tone.

"Yes, that and a whole lot more." My answer amuses Jeremey. But I follow up with a question of my

104

own. "I suspect that you do not believe God exists, so if He doesn't exist, what would be your explanation?"

Jeremey is ready and answers.

"Everything is the product of chance. You are right, neither the blind man nor his parents are at fault. They simply have the misfortune of experiencing the randomness of chance. I think of it as fate, and some call it karma. But in the end, they were just not lucky enough to experience good. I am sure they probably all wished he had never been born instead of having to live life with that infirmity."

"So you assume, it would have been better for the man never to have been born, than to discover at the age of thirty or so, suddenly you would have the sight you had been denied as a youth, and then have all of the other experiences that would occur after that event?" My question causes Jeremey to pause.

"No, obviously if your story were true, then the man had a future that might make up for his past misfortune, but it's a fairy tale, and not everything in life ends with a happy ending." Jeremey smirking tone is one of victory in the argument.

"You are wrong, and you are right. You don't know the end of the blind man's story. He gets married and has several children. They are forced to flee the country and end up in Gaul, which is now call France, and then migrate across the channel to Britannia which we now call England. They work there among the Picts, one of the tribes that the Romans are trying to conquer. There, one of his children would betray both his wife and him, and they would both be put to death. So, the end of their lives was even more brutal than the beginning. A person they loved, who was a part of their family, was the cause of their deaths.

"In that way, you are right, his life did not have a happy ending in this world. But they would not have changed a thing they experienced. And his words in the story your wife just read are what brought me to faith. I

105

am eternally grateful that he experienced that blindness, because the good that came out of it has changed so many lives that I suspect it is a number too vast to number. It was his voice, his experience that finally penetrated my heart of stone. Also, while I know you don't believe this yet, I fully expect to be able to thank him for his words and the testimony that led me to Jesus, and then, you will know just how wrong you were, when you see the joy he is now experiencing."

Jeremey is still shaking his head, but I turn to Jonathan. "You have another question Jonathan, don't you?" Jonathan nods, looking first at his father, who is still shaking his head, and then at his mom.

"Go ahead, honey; you can ask your question," Kathryn says, encouraging her son. It is obvious Jonathan has already asked his next question of his mom. I wish I knew her answer, but I am praying I can answer it truthfully.

"Why would God give me a tumor that is going to kill me? What good can come from that? What's God's purpose for this and for my life?"

Jonathan's tone is one of sadness and expectation mixed. I see out of the corner of my eye, Jeremey's head has stopped shaking, and a tenseness has suddenly appeared through his body as well. He is coiled like a spring, ready to pop, but he is waiting my answer. I finally find my voice, having been praying silently for wisdom to give my answer.

"Jonathan, I do not know why God has allowed you to have a tumor. I also cannot see the good that is going to come from it. But I know that everything that happens God is involved in, so that His person will be glorified by everything and everyone. "

I go on, telling them my own story, the loss of my first wife, and our daughter. My role in the death of my daughter, and the great blessings that followed, with Carol, my second wife, and my daughter Laura. I hide nothing, hoping that in my story perhaps I can provide

106

an inkling of what the answers are to Jonathan's questions.

"So, you see, I don't have the answers to your questions about your life; all I can do is talk to you about my own life, and the answers I have come to about my own experiences. I don't know completely why I was spared death when I had my stroke, or what His purpose was in giving me the experience of the stroke, or why I am now living with an aneurism that may at any moment end my life, but I know Jesus is involved in every detail, and that together with the Father and the Spirit, they are working it all out for good."

Jeremey's head is back to shaking, and he stands looking at me.

"You don't have answers, just parables and musings about your own life. Jeremey has a tumor because something caused it that we have not figured out yet. When we do figure it out, and we will, no other person will ever need to experience it again. I'm making it my mission in life to ensure that I develop my skills to the point that I will never fail again. No other family should ever have to experience what we are. In the meantime, I'm not going to waste anymore of my time listening to this nonsense."

He turns toward the door but looks back at his wife.

"Kathryn, I am going home. I hope you and Jonathan will come home soon as well. He has no answers for us."

Before Jeremey fully opens the door, I ask a parting question.

"What would it take for you to consider whether the story in the Bible is real and whether the blind man's testimony is true?" I ask.

Jeremey turns slightly, and answers, his voice a combination of sarcasm and anger. "A Miracle."

And then he is gone.

107

On the chair where he was sitting is the pouch and the coin. He has left it.

I turn back to Kathryn and Jonathan. It is Kathryn who speaks first.

"I'm sorry, Rubin. We didn't mean to put you through that. It was just our hope that perhaps something would change his thoughts."

I look at Jonathan.

"I'm sorry I didn't have better answers for your questions, Jonathan. It's strange, you know. We think when a person gets old, like me, that somehow these things that happen are more to be expected, but when things happen to someone young like you, the answers to the questions should have firmer understandable answers. But the answer to both of our circumstances is the same.

"God is a weaver; we get to see our lives as one of those threads being woven into the tapestry He is creating. We see the tapestry from the back side, and at times it looks like a bundle of knots and frizzy threads. But every so often we get a glimpse of the front side, and when we see that, we are startled at the sheer beauty of what is being created. All I can tell you for sure is that your life has meaning and purpose. He created you through your mother and father. And all that He intends is still mysterious and unknown, but I do know this. When you finally see your life story in that tapestry, it will be beautiful, and your thread is indispensable to that tapestry."

At that moment, the door opens again, and there are four people coming back into the room. Laura sees the pouch on Carol's chair and picks it up, bringing it over to Jonathan and sliding it over his head. Jonathan slides the pouch back under his T-shirt. Even Sue is back, looking as though she has had a full night of sleep, but I know she has now been up for over twenty-eight hours. They each return to their seats, and it is Louis who asks the first question.

108

"Would you like to tell us how the conversation with Dr. Baine went?"

I spend five minutes, trying to sum up the conversation. I end with Jeremey's requirement for considering the truthfulness of the story. "A Miracle," I say, ending the summary. Jonathan nods, but Kathryn is looking at the floor, as if afraid to meet anyone's eyes. I know how difficult this must be for her. Yet, she is still here. It is Jonathan who brings us all back together.

"Mr. Rubin, I would like to hear more of the story, if you don't mind?" His words cause me to pause from jumping into the rabbit hole my mind was about to.

I look over at Laura, and she is already reorganizing the pages, and I see she is ready to return to the task at hand.

"Sure, Jonathan, I think that will be good for us to do," I say, waiting for Laura to take over. She doesn't disappoint, and soon again we are again journeying with Lazarus and hearing the rest of his story.

Chapter Twelve - Three Friends – Three Deaths – Three Miracles

"Caleb and his mother lived in Nain, a good day's journey from Nazareth. The small village was just slightly smaller than Bethany, and like Bethany, it was on the ascent coming up from the valley between Mount Moriah and the village. Caleb's father had died when Caleb turned sixteen. His father often would go to nearby villages to collect fruits and other vegetables not found in the immediate vicinity of Nain. His father had decided to go to Cana to bring back some of the grapes of that region, to sell in their stall in Nain. Some travelers found his body less than a mile from Nain, and from what they could tell, he had fallen down one of the many steep inclines scattered throughout the region. Nothing pointed to anything but an accident, as the money he had taken with him was found still with his body.

Caleb's father had taught him how to buy and sell different fruits and vegetables, and that trade from the small stall in the market at Nain had provided for both he and his mother for the years prior to his father's death. Now, it provided a meager but sustainable life for them both. But all of that was about to change. Caleb had suffered through various illnesses before, but this one was different. After more than a week of illness, the coughing had increased and breathing became much more difficult. When he coughed now great globs of yellowish-green material also came up. He lasted another two days, and early in the morning on the day before the Sabbath, he died.

Caleb shared his experience with me when he came with Ruth, seeking me out, to share his own experience and to compare his experience to both Ruth's and mine. His story and experiences where remarkably similar in many ways. He told me his story, and I will try and tell it the way he told me.

111

Laura's voice changed. A slightly higher tone, the change caused Kathryn and Sue to look at me in concern, but I motioned with my hand that it was okay. I had experienced this before, as the voice she was now portraying was of a different witness, not the same person who had been speaking was now talking. We went back to listening, and soon returned to the story.

For my mother, my death was even more traumatic than the loss of my father. I was the only means she had for support, and there was no other family in Nain for her to turn to. With the Sabbath so close, and with the rules regulating burial of those who had died so explicit, neighbors had stepped in to help my mother prepare my body for burial.

Around Nain, along many of the steep inclines leading into the village are many caves. These caves have served as burial places for many generations for the people of Nain. My father's bones, and those of his parents resided in one, and it was there they were taking my body for burial. On the way out of the city, the funeral procession was met by a large crowd of people who were following Jesus, the teacher/healer who was becoming even better known for healing so many sick people and driving spirits out of others. He stopped the procession. My mother and many of the neighbors were weeping, the sorrow of my death and the unknown future breaking her heart. Jesus's words to her were, "Do not weep." Walking over to the open casket they were using to transport my body to the grave site, I heard his voice when he said, "Young man, I say to you arise."

Immediately, I returned. There was quite a commotion going on, as people were exclaiming that "A great prophet has arisen among us" and others were crying out "God has visited his people." In general, there was fear and wonderment among the people from the village. But for my mother, inexpressible joy as she touched the sides of my face and wept now for joy. It would only be when I was alone with my mother, that

112

she would ask the questions, that no one had dared to ask. "What do you remember? What did it feel like when you returned?"

I answered her second question first. I told her the first thing I realized was that my breathing was completely normal. In fact, it was better than it had been before I became ill. The crushing heaviness of the illness was gone, and my sides no longer ached from the coughing exertion I had experienced when I was sick. I shared the surprise I felt when I sat up, suddenly seeing again, and remembering how ill I had been, and realizing that I felt as if I had slept a sound sleep and was now completely refreshed. The first question would take me much longer to process and put together my thoughts. I was sure people would think I was crazy, and I did not want to burden my mother with what I remembered.

Shortly after Jesus had brought me back, I heard the rumors circulating in the village, that I had not really died but had merely swooned. There was a belief that the spirits of those who were dying might exist just outside the body, and simply decide to come back, and not leave, so even the ones assumed to have died, may not have actually died. I should not have feared what my mother might think. She had seen death before, and she knew I had died.

I never had to challenge those who were saying such things, for my mother did it for me. "The prophet, Jesus, raised my son from death and gave him back to me." That statement would silence all the foolish talk of something else having occurred, at least while she was present. My booth in the market became swamped with visitors, everyone seeking me out to talk to me about the experience. While the attention would slowly fade, for more than a year people would stop by to see if what they had heard was true. My mother always told the same story, and most people would just stare at me with appreciation. But there were others who did not

113

appreciate what my mother would willingly testify to.

After Jesus was killed in Jerusalem, and when we heard his disciples were now saying he had risen, my mother made the decision for us. "We need to go to Jerusalem, to be among his disciples, so we can learn what has happened."

We came to Jerusalem and stayed there many days. Ruth also arrived there, drawn as we had been by the events she was hearing about from her home in Capernaum. She was only turning fifteen by this time, but her father Jairus and her mother accompanied her to Jerusalem, where we met.

We were there for the festival of Pentecost about five days after we arrived, and we heard Peter speak. But Lazarus was already gone, as the people who had taken Jesus's life were looking for him as well. His miracle was one they had no explanation for, and just his presence challenged the stories they were telling about Jesus.

For almost three years we sat under the apostles' teaching. When Stephen was killed, and the persecution broke out in Jerusalem, I returned with my mother to Nain, and Ruth went with her parents back to Capernaum. It was two years later when we learned where Lazarus had gone, and by then, both Ruth and I needed to talk with him.

Laura's voice changes again, and she is back in the tone of the earlier part of the story.

When Caleb and Ruth found me, Caleb wanted to talk about what he remembered after he died, and before he was called back to life. He spoke of his conversation with his father in that place and was surprised that his father was the first person he met, learning that his father was still very much present, but just not in his former place. He spoke also of two men who were there, but not like the rest of the people he met. He knew something was different about them, and recognized one as a prophet, but there had not been enough time for

114

him to hear their stories. And there was light in that place that filled every corner so that no shadows or darkness existed there. It was that light that he most wanted to share and hear whether I had experienced the same. He told me the most difficult thing about returning, was leaving that light. In that matter, what he and Ruth and I had experienced was remarkably similar. Ruth's story though just added even more confirmation that Jesus was something far greater than being just a prophet.

Ruth lived in Capernaum close to the Lake of Gennesaret, also known by more common names as the Sea of Galilee or Sea of Tiberias. The lake is massive and filled with fish. But the water is beautiful, and it is one of the reasons Ruth fell in love with the island where I have lived more than forty years. I believe the water reminded her of her home, and in my mind's eye I can see her still running along the shoreline, rejoicing in the glory of the water. Her time with me seems to have been but a blink of an eye, but for twenty years we often walked together on the water's edge, and I still see her joy as she took in that panoramic view.

Many of the people who lived near Lake Gennesaret were involved in the fishing business. Peter and his brother Andrew both worked with their father in that business, and Andrew would meet Jesus there and bring his brother Peter to also meet Jesus. It would be only a short time later that Jesus would call the two brothers from their work on the boat with their father and tell them they would be "fishers of men" going forward. Even Mathew the tax collector lived there, as Capernaum was also a center of commerce, and Rome had set up the town as a center for the gathering of taxes as well. Jesus often visited the area, and many people met the preacher/healer during his stays there.

Ruth was a young girl, only about twelve when she fell gravely ill. It happened so suddenly, her father, Jairus, had no time to seek out other physicians. It was

115

obvious to him and his wife that their daughter was dying before their eyes.

Now Jairus was serving as a leader in the synagogue there. This was the same synagogue the Roman centurion had built for the Jewish community there and who had experienced the healing of his own servant by Jesus earlier. So Jairus knew of that miracle, and he knew Jesus was returning to Capernaum. He left his wife and servants caring for his daughter and went to find Jesus. It took more than two hours, as Jairus's home was close to the lake, and a distance from both the synagogue and from the road that curved around the hill and into the town. Ruth's father found Jesus just outside the town, walking with a large crowd of people, including his disciples, toward Capernaum.

Ruth remembered her father talking about the encounter and explaining how large the crowd was and the difficulty he had reaching Jesus. When he did finally reach Jesus, he had knelt to the ground before him and said, "My daughter, my only child, is near death, please come and lay your hands on her and heal her." The crowd was so large and so noisy that Ruth's father was afraid Jesus might not have heard his petition and repeated the words again. By the time he repeated it the second time, his eyes had filled with tears, and they were dripping down his face.

Jesus had reached down and taken Ruth's father by the arm and lifted him up. "I will go with you," Jesus said. But the crowd was so large with people both in front and behind Jesus the progress was painfully slow. The crowd was jostling one another, everyone looking to be as close to Jesus as possible. One woman had been pushing her way closer to Jesus and finally had reached out from behind and touched Jesus's cloak. At that touch, Jesus had stopped and begun looking around at the people. Jairus was anxious to keep moving, but he stopped waiting for Jesus to begin moving again.

"Who is the one who touched me?" Jesus asked.

116

Peter, who was close to Jesus, looked at the crowd and responded, "Master, the people are crowding and pressing in on you." Peter's statement was true, many were bumping into Jesus.

But Jesus continued to look around saying, "Someone did touch me, as I was aware that power had gone out of me." Jesus was not looking for all the ones who had bumped into him, but the one person who had a need and reached out to him to fill that need.

Finally, the women fell at his feet and confessed her healing. She had been struggling for more than twelve years with her monthly cycle that never seemed to stop. She had been to numerous doctors and had spent much of her wealth seeking to be healed. In desperation and hope, she had sought out Jesus, thinking "If I only touch his cloak, I will be healed. He doesn't even need to pay attention to me or do anything special about me."

Jesus smiled at the woman, telling her, "Daughter, your faith has made you well, go in peace."

Jesus was still speaking with the woman when one of Jairus's neighbors reached the group as well. Pulling Jairus aside, the neighbor said, "Your daughter has died; do not trouble the teacher anymore."

Jesus heard what the neighbor said and told Jairus, "Do not be afraid any longer; only believe and she will be made well."

Ruth told me her father later talked of this moment as when he was tested the most. He remembered the miracle of the centurion's servant, but that servant had been sick but had not died. He had just heard the testimony of the woman who also had experienced the power of Jesus. She had touched him and had been made well. He heard Jesus's words, but doubt and sadness almost overwhelmed him. He thought about his wife, alone and dealing with this event on her own. He thought about Ruth, and tears leaked from his eyes as he turned and continued the journey back to his home. What would be find there?

117

It took Jairus almost another half hour to reach his home with Jesus and the crowd that was still following Jesus. When he reached his home many neighbors and friends stood outside the house, and from the inside of the home the sound of weeping and even wailing could be heard. Jairus's wife came outside, tears flowing down her face, and seeing her husband, collapsed into his arms. Jesus spoke briefly with his disciples and instructed that they keep the crowd away from the home. Turning to Peter, John, and James, he asked them to come into the house with him. Jesus put his arm around Jairus and helped him and his wife into their home. The neighbors and friends in the house were either weeping or talking about Ruth and how sad it was that such a young person had died. Jesus stunned many of the mourners when he commanded, "Stop weeping, for she has not died, but is asleep."

A group of the neighbors began to sarcastically laugh at his comment, as they had seen death before, and it was obvious Ruth was dead. Jesus looked around at the group and asked his three disciples to move the crowd to the outside. Now the room where Ruth was laying was separated by a curtain from the main room in the house. When the people had been moved out of the house, the disciples returned, and then Jesus took Jairus, his wife, and the three disciples into the room where Ruth was.

Ruth's father would tell Ruth how motionless she had been, lying there on the bed. Her chest was not moving as it normally would when sleeping. Her eyes were closed, and there was no sound coming from her. He would confess this was all the moment when all his doubts flooded over him, as he, too, had seen death before, and certainly his daughter was dead.

Yet what happened next would forever change Jairus, his wife, and Ruth.

Ruth remembered she heard the words clearly. "Talitha kum." The words were said as a command, and

118

instantly she felt the need to stand and embrace the one who called her. Ruth remembered the look on her father and mother's faces as she took the hand of the caller, and he helped her to her feet, and then seeing her parents, she smiled.

Almost immediately she also realized the tiredness, weakness, and breathing troubles she had been experiencing before were gone, and she was incredibly hungry. The man who held her hand seemed to understand this final need, as he told her parents they should keep what had happened to themselves, but that they needed to give her some food. It was her mother who found the bread and piece of fish, and gave it to her, and Ruth admitted that at first, she only took small bites but then ate the food, feeling famished.

After the man left her with the three other men, Ruth asked what had happened and who the man was. Her father told her of his seeking the healer, Jesus, and then shared everything that had happened. Many neighbors returned, questioning her parents, and Ruth constantly heard her father say, "Jesus, the healer, touched my daughter and healed her." Ruth listened as many other questions were asked and even asked some herself before the evening came.

She was finally tired and ready for sleep. It would be her mother who would ask the first question of Ruth as she prepared for sleep. "What do you remember?"

She would recount to her mother, and later to Caleb and me, the place of great light, and being told by several people there that she must wait, for her time with them was for but a short time. Like Caleb, she, too, remembered the feeling of the light filling every fiber of her being, and the light was more than just light, it was filled with life.

That experience would become the driving force that led both her and Caleb to seek out me, the only other person to have experienced this type of miracle. As would be expected, the story began to circulate about

119

Ruth as well, that she had not really died, but instead had only swooned. But my miracle would be something different. The stench of death is not one easily forgotten, or easily explained away.

After the healing of Cain, Jesus had left Bethany, as both he and his followers knew the religious leaders were looking for any opportunity to seize him. It was only two months before the Passover celebration and already pilgrims were making their way to Jerusalem. The ruffian who had punched Cain so many years ago was now a man and was caught up in another of the endless insurrections that occurred against the Romans. Barabbas was waiting judgement in the Roman prison, and it was known that the governor wanted to make a spectacle of the man. These were just a few of the events that would serve as the backdrop against the experience I was about to have.

I had been working very long hours, and the business was prospering beyond anything I expected. The olive oil and wine from the groves had increased every year and the demand for the spices and perfumes continued to increase as well. I was busy and happy, and the stories about my friend the carpenter-turned-healer also were increasing by the day.

It seemed every Sabbath, when I would be either in the local synagogue or at the temple, everyone was talking about Jesus. Some of the discussions were very disturbing, because the arguments about whether Jesus was a real prophet or some type of imposter were increasing. One of the Pharisees, a man named Nikodemus, had tried to defend Jesus, only to be shouted down by others who asked, "has any prophet ever come from Nazareth?"

As I returned home from that Sabbath worship, I realized I was not feeling well. By the morning, I was not able to rise from my bed. Both of my sisters found me with a very high fever and a cough that was racking my frame. They brought me several herbal drinks, made

120

from the spices we used for medicinal purposes, but nothing was appearing to help me. I had long believed that sleep was the best cure for any illness, but even though I slept much of the next three days, nothing I did seemed to make a difference.

Both Mary and Martha were more than concerned. I would later learn they had drafted a message to Jesus, and asked Nathan, who was now as much a brother as a servant, if he would take the message to Jesus who was more than a day away from Bethany. It was Martha who penned the short note that said: "Lord, behold, he whom You love is sick."

I was already too delirious and weak from both the fever and the coughing to know much of what was happening. The few hours when I was alert, I spent pleading with God that I might be allowed to get better. I worried about my sisters, and I wondered how they would manage if I did not get better. I continued to struggle on, but three days after my sisters had sent the message to Jesus, and at least two days after he received the note, I awoke in the morning with the realization that I was having even greater difficulty breathing. Both my sisters were there, and I looked at them. I remember Mary's hand running the damp cloth against my forehead, and Martha holding one of my hands.

My voice was incredibly weak, but I remember looking at them both and whispering, "I love you," and then I closed my eyes. My sisters would tell me much later, that after I spoke those three words, I simply stopped breathing.

I have heard others speak of being able to witness the commotion associated with their own death. Both Ruth and Caleb had memories of some of the activities going on around them when they died. I do not. Instead, I closed my eyes there on that bed and opened my eyes again to see the smiling faces of my father and mother who had been waiting for me, against the backdrop of the brightest place I had ever experienced. The light did

121

not cause me to squint, like if you were looking straight at the sun, but instead this light seemed to cause everything to look crisper and clearer, with more vibrant color than any experience I had before. My four days there were glorious, and the realization that I could not stay pulled on me, although at the same time I knew I was being giving a glimpse at something most people would have given everything they owned to see.

Much of what would happen the next four days in Bethany, comes from my sisters and their memory of the events. Although Mary was often thought of as the more spiritually mature woman, it was Martha who took over the responsibilities of preparing everything for my burial. Nathan had returned with the news that he had been successful in delivering the message, and he and his wife had been constantly at our home helping both of my sisters in taking care of their needs.

It was Martha who told Nathan the news that I had died. He took on the responsibilities of preparing my body for burial and used the oils and perfumes from our stock to anoint my body. The amount of spices and perfumes used would easily consume a week's worth of wages for the average family. But for my family, it barely scratched the supply we had on hand. Nathan's wife had bought the linen she tore into long strips, giving those to her husband, who had then gently wrapped my body after the oils and perfumes had been applied. Over my face they laid a single cloth that was also infused with special oils and spices as well.

Like Caleb, they placed my body into a woven casket, and then transported my body to the same tomb where my parents and grandparents rested as well. It was Cain, who learning of my death brought the clay jars from his father's business that he would use to arrange the bones of my parents and place those jars next to the jars containing my grandparents' bones before my body was laid on the same shelf I had place my father's body on more than ten years earlier.

122

Together Nathan and Cain rolled the stone covering the cave back in place after my body rested in that tomb.

Mary had been almost unreconcilable. If not for the presence of Cain, her sorrow would likely have broken her. Our family was so well known, and I believe respected and loved, that a crowd of neighbors, mostly women, came and stayed with Mary and Martha. The seven families who cared for the vineyards and groves all were there. For four long days the mourning continued, not realizing that my perspective was filled with anything but sorrow.

It is a tradition among us that when we are in mourning, we wear clothing set aside for that purpose. I do not know where that tradition came from, but both my sisters had face veils that would hide their faces so their deep emotions were hidden when the sorrow of what had happened would sweep over them. Both my sisters had times of impossible sorrow, and the friends who meant well actually added to the atmosphere of grief.

For four days, both my sisters heard the stories told from neighbors' perspectives about my life. There was much laughter but even more tears. It is hard for me to express what was happening to my sisters. How do you explain the loss of a family member until you have experienced that for yourself?

We had experienced the loss of our parents, but we three had experienced that together. There was something even more devastating for my sisters when I died. There had always been the three of us, and now there were only two. Neither of my sisters were married yet, and in God's providence, Jesus had healed Cain first so he could be there when Mary needed that support the most.

On the fourth day after my death, a neighbor came and told my sisters Jesus was coming. Once again it was Martha who left our home and went to meet Jesus on the path coming to Bethany. She found him, falling at

123

his feet and saying, "Lord, if you had been here, my brother would not have died. Even now I know that whatever You ask of God, God will give you."

Jesus had reach down and drawn her up to her feet. Jesus said to her, "Your brother will rise again."

She responded to Jesus believing he was accepting the point of view of the Pharisees. "I know that he will rise again in the resurrection on the last day."

Jesus's response might have surprised others, but Martha was not taken back when he said, "I am the resurrection and the life; he who believes in Me will live even if he dies, and everyone who lives and believes in Me will never die. Do you believe this?"

Martha's response would show just how far she had come in her own understanding and awareness of who Jesus, the carpenter's son and our friend, really was. When I would later hear of her words, I would be surprised how much further she had come, than even I had come. She answered Jesus saying, "Yes, Lord, I have believed that You are the Christ, the Son of God, even He who comes into the world." In that brief statement, Martha revealed how much more she understood, and it would take what would happen shortly for me to also embrace that declaration.

Jesus looked at Martha and asked, "Where is Mary?"

Martha said, "I will get her."

Our home was more than twenty minutes away from where Martha had found Jesus. When she reached our home, she discovered Mary still in our meeting area, which served, as well, as our dining area. Many cloaks and robes rested on the table that Jesus and Joseph had made. Our neighbors and friends were still talking, although Mary was sitting in one of the corners, away from everyone else.

Martha bent down to Mary and whispered, "The teacher is here and is calling for you."

124

Mary still had on the same set of clothes she had worn since the day of the funeral. She had slept little, but she immediately rose and left the room with Martha closely following. All of the people in the home saw Mary leaving quickly, and they assumed she was going to the tomb to grieve there. It was often the case that the family members of the dead person would return to the tomb to weep there. So it was a large group of people who followed at a short distance as my two sisters made their way to where Jesus was waiting. Amazingly, Jesus had not moved from the spot where Martha had first met him. His disciples would later tell us he had closed his eyes and had been silently praying, and all of the people following Jesus had left him alone.

When Mary reached Jesus, she repeated Martha's example and collapsed at his feet saying, "Lord, if you had been here, my brother would not have died."

Those words broke the dam that had limited her tears, and again sorrow dripped from her eyes. The crowd of neighbors and friends also had many who were crying, and even some of the men who had cared for the vineyards and groves were crying. Jesus reached down and helped Mary to her feet. Seeing her great sorrow and the display of grief coming from the crowd that had followed Mary and Martha caused a deep well of emotion to spring up from within Jesus, to the point that his body shook.

Looking at Mary and then Martha he asked, "Where have you laid him?"

Martha answered, "Lord come and see."

Jesus wept.

I have long wondered why he wept. I know he was connected to the emotions that flooded over my sisters and the people who were with them. But I now know he already knew what he was about to do. I believe he was seeing far beyond my death and the sorrow it was bringing. He had been there when that first act of

125

disobedience brought death and sadness to us all, and he was already looking ahead to the fulfilling of the promise he had made and the price he would pay to finally be able to put an end to all death and sorrow

Cain was there as well, following Mary, to be there for her. He heard some in the crowd of people saying to one another, "See how he loved him." Still others, seeing Cain among them said, "Could not this man who opened the eyes of the blind man have also kept this man from dying?" Even now, in one breath some of the crowd was speaking of one miracle while criticizing Jesus for not being there to perform another. All of those doubters were about to witness something never seen before.

Coming to the cave serving as the tomb, Jesus said, "Remove the stone."

That request brought gasps from the crowd, and already some moved farther away from the tomb. Martha approached Jesus, and said, "Lord, by this time there will be a stench, for he has been dead for four days." Her words had been said softly, almost reverently, attempting to prevent further sorrow. Mary's face had paled at the suggestion of opening the tomb.

Jesus looked at Martha and spoke directly to her. He connected with her earlier confession and said, "Did I not say to you that if you believed, you would see the glory of God?" His words were said in tenderness but with an authority that caused Martha to step back, next to where Mary was already standing.

Cain and Nathan came forward again and moved the stone that four days ago they had placed in front of the entrance to the grave.

One of the facts that would cause so many to want to also put me to death again, was the odor that emerged when that stone was taken away. There was absolutely no doubt—within the tomb, death was present. The sweet smell of the perfumes and spices could not completely hide the other smell that was

126

undeniable. Even as those odors crept from the grave, Jesus looked upward and spoke in words that many heard clearly. "Father, I thank you that you have heard me. I knew that you always hear Me; but because of the people standing around I said it, so that they may believe that You sent me."

Then with a loud voice he called out, "Lazarus, come forth."

I heard that voice as clearly as I have ever heard anything. Even from the great distance where I stood, that call was clear, undeniable, and a command that was to be obeyed immediately. My first memory was of the muted light filtering through the spice-infused cloth they had placed over my face. But there was also another smell the fragrances could not hide, but it was a putrid stench that was rapidly fading, as if it were being blown away even as I sat up and then stood. There was a breeze swirling around my body, and I felt warmth and life flowing through my body. Every nerve was tingling as my body returned to activity.

My body was covered with the linen material used for such occurrences, but while I could walk, I couldn't move my arms to free myself. His voice was still echoing in my mind and came from the other side of the opening I walked to.

I emerged into the light of what I guessed must have been the middle of the day. I sensed there were many people there, as I heard their gasps. I immediately recognized the cries of recognition that were coming from my sisters. And then I heard his voice again, "Unbind him and let him go."

Laura stops again, just as the door to my room opens again. I am surprised we have been able to listen undisturbed for so long. It has been at least two hours since my last poking and prodding experience. But this time it is Dr. Charles who is holding the door open and surveying the collection of people all sitting and obviously listening to my daughter Laura. Laura takes the last page she has read and lays it carefully on the pile

127

of paper beside her. The stack that remains on her lap is noticeably smaller than the stack to her side.

When Dr, Charles steps in I realize Mildred from the CT Scanning is also with him. "Sorry to disturb you all," he says, and then turning to me he continues, "Rubin, we need to take another scan, to see if the medicines I prescribed did anything." It is also at that moment that he sees both Jonathan and Kathryn as well. "Jonathan, Kathryn, what are you doing here? I thought you were all at your home with Jeremey." The question is asked in genuine surprise. It is Kathryn who answers his question.

"Yes, we were home, but Jonathan wanted to hear more of the story Laura was reading to Rubin, so we came back for that."

Dr. Charles looks again at Laura, and at the piles of paper neatly arranged beside her, and on her lap. He smiles, but then says, "Mildred tells me we have a window of time to squeeze you in for the next forty-five minutes or so, and I really need to take advantage of that opportunity." I am struck again with the note of familiarity in Dr. Charles's voice, as if he and Mildred have a long and friendly relationship. I like this doctor more every time I meet him, and it is obvious that Mildred also respects him, by the way she is looking at the doctor. I nod, and turning to Carol I say, "Perhaps you all can stay here and talk, while I go get this test done?"

Carol takes up the conversation, and soon Mildred is pushing my bed out of the room. But Dr. Charles is not following her, and the door closes solidly once my bed clears the door. I look at Mildred, but I can tell she is waiting until we are in a more private setting to say anything to me. Once we are in the elevator, she asks the first question.

"What's your daughter reading that has so many people interested in hearing? Even Jonathan who is so sick. I did not think I would ever see him again." We

128

talk for the entire trip to the CT scanning room, and then I once again get to experience the tube, the clunking and the music, but this time I am praying for everyone who is hearing the story. I wonder what questions are being asked and answered back in my hospital room. But I know both Carol and Laura are quite capable of answering the questions. It's just that I would like to be there as well, to hear the questions.

I begin praying again holding what I know of the struggles of each person listening to the story, but especially for Jonathan and Jeremey, who both need a miracle. I'm in the middle of my prayer asking for a miracle for Jeremey, when I feel the dizziness begin. "Mildred!" I cry out, and then the world goes from gray to black.

Chapter Thirteen – What's in a Miracle?

For the second time, I awake, but this time the room is not the same. I feel the strange sensation of my head being cold. I can sense the head covering but know instantly that my sparse hair is no longer present on my head. I try to raise my arms but discover they are tied down. Instantly, a nurse is hovering over me, and it is a new nurse, not one I know.

"Mr. James, can you hear me?"

My eyes must have gone wild for an instant, as my mind was trying to process everything, the new location and sensations. The feeling of restraint is never one I have accepted well. Slowly I gather my thoughts, and I feel my galloping heartbeat slowing down. Then Dr. Charles comes into my view. He is dressed head to as far as I can see in surgical outfit. His hands have the unmistakable gloves and there is a lite pink hue to those. His face is hidden by the surgical mask, but I recognize his eyes.

"Rubin, can you hear me?" he asks.

I try to nod my head, but even my head feels restrained as well.

"Yes," I answer, and my voice sounds strained and like it is coming from a great distance. "What happened?" I try asking, but I hear the words, and it sounds something like "at haped." It's like my vocal cords have forgotten how to form the sounds, and then everything fades again.

I don't know how long it is, but when I open my eyes again, it appears I am in a different room, but not the original room I remember, nor the second room. I turn my head, and discover my head is no longer restrained, but the sensation of having a hat on, remains. I try to move my arms and find they, too, are no longer restrained, but I can see a bazillion wires connected to my arms and to my chest.

Another nurse is there again, another new one.

131

"Welcome back, Mr. James. I'm Paula Jones, and I need to tell Dr. Browning you are awake."

I hear her move to another location in the room and hear her on some form of a communication system.

"Doctor, Mr. James is awake. Yes, I will tell him that. Yes, I understand. I will stay here and monitor him. "

Paula is back and looking down on me. I feel, well how do I put it, weird. While Paula was talking, I was taking stock of everything. I can feel my fingers and toes, and I practice wiggling them. As far as I can tell, everything is moving, although my one leg still feels like a weight is keeping it firmly on the bed. My rear end aches like it has been in this position for too long. I try to move my body, to take some of the pressure of that area, but Paula is right there.

"Mr. James, you shouldn't try and move just yet."

Her words strike a nerve in me, and I bite my tongue. Literally. I have learned that it is the only way for me to keep unpleasantries from erupting from my mouth. I learned to form that habit, which now occurs almost without me thinking, back when I finally came to my senses about myself. It was one of the changes within me when I finally came to the truth I had been rejecting for so many years.

Finally, I know I have mastered my emotion, and I say, "My bottom hurts."

Paula is there, again, and she expertly slides her hands and arms under my backsides and gently rolls me a little so my bottom is now at a different angle. The relief is almost instantaneous.

"Thank you," I say.

I realize my words, while softly said, at least make sense to me. Paula obviously understands because she answers. "You're welcome."

From this new position I can see several of the monitors to the side of the bed, and I realize I am not lying flat, but instead, the upper half of my body

132

appears to be slightly raised.

I'm about to ask Paula another question when I hear the door to the room open, and the smiling face of Dr. Charles Browning is in my line of sight. He is no longer dressed in his surgical suit, but in the traditional while trench coat that identifies him as a medical professional.

"Hi, Rubin," he says. "Welcome back."

I am sure I am smiling, but the need to know what has happened has filled my thoughts.

"Where did I go?" is my response.

Dr. Charles laughs at that.

"Well, you gave us quite a scare. The vein in your head, well it ruptured while you were in the CT scan. When Mildred called me, we had you in surgery less than two minutes after it started bleeding. Let's just say, we tried something new, and it appears that it may have worked."

I understand, although it takes me a few minutes to put the pieces together. Both Jonathan's father, Dr. Baine, and Dr. Charles had told me if the aneurism ruptured, there was nothing they could do to save me. But here I am, still alive, at least for the moment.

"Can I see my wife?" I ask.

Dr. Charles doesn't answer right away, but then says: "Yes, Rubin, I will let her know you are awake. But you are not out of the woods yet. What I tried bought us some time, but it's not a cure, just a stalling motion. I just want to be sure you understand. "

I do. What Dr. Charles has just told me is, the death sentence has not been commuted, only delayed. He wants to be sure I understand.

"How long?" I ask.

"I don't know. What we are trying has never been done before. It may be minutes or months. I simply don't know. Frankly, it is a miracle you are still with us," he says,

There is that word, miracle.

133

I know the definition: an extraordinary event manifesting divine intervention in human affairs, but I also understand that often the word is used to describe events not expected. Dr. Charles was trying something new on me that had never been done before. The fact that it has worked has surprised him to the point he feels the outcome was unexpected, and that I am still here is in his mind a miracle. Is that a "divine intervention?" I do know Christ is always present and active in everything that occurs. Whether this was a special intervention, I do not know, but I am grateful, nonetheless.

I had expected Dr. Charles to leave, to find Carol, but he doesn't. Instead he gets closer to me and asks, "What did you do to Jonathan?" I am truly confused now. The last I saw of Jonathan he was with his mother and the rest of us listening to Laura read the manuscript she had translated.

"Is Jonathan okay?" I asked, expecting the worst news, that he had died like I almost had. But Dr. Charles's smile is out of place for something as sobering as his death.

"Yes, Jonathan is okay. In fact, he is better than okay. A lot has happened in the three days you have been in your own crisis."

He goes on explaining that while I was still in the CT Scan, almost at the instant the vein in my brain burst, Jonathan had collapsed, falling out of the wheelchair he was sitting in beside his mother. Dr. Charles was still in the room, as was my night-time nurse, Sue, and together they had rushed Jonathan downstairs, thinking the worst. By the time they got to the CT room, Mildred was already frantically removing me from the scanner and had already put out the call for Dr. Charles. Providence put him in front of her even before she had been able to move me out the scanner. She had explained to Dr. Charles what was happening.

He had made the decision, having checked Jonathan's breathing and vitals, and turned his care

134

over to Mildred while he and Sue rushed me to the operating room. Dr. Charles had called several other nurses and specialists to the surgical center, and unbeknownst to me, seven medical professionals were assisting Dr. Charles as he attempted the new procedure. After more than four hours of surgery, I had come around briefly, for that short exchange, before I had once again blacked out. I was in the surgery area for more than thirteen hours, and then Dr. Charles had done everything he could, to save my life.

"When I emerged from the surgery on you, Mildred was waiting. She had the CT scan for Jonathan. She told me, 'Jonathan is awake, and has been eating and talking almost nonstop for the past eight hours, Doctor.' Mildred said, 'I looked at the scan, but thought it had to be a mistake, so I ran it again.' She gave me the second CT scan as well. I examined both and compared it to the CT scan of a week ago. All three scans are definitely of Jonathan, but while the one from a week ago showed the massive invasion of that cancerous tumor, on the new scans, the tumor...well it's gone."

"Gone?" I ask again, to be sure I had heard him correctly.

"Yes, gone. There is not even a trace or a shadow of what had been there a week ago. It's like it was never there. What did you do Rubin?"

I am thinking about the timing, everything we had been hearing Laura read, and then thinking about my last prayers before that vein in my head exploded. Finally, I am ready to answer.

"All I did, Doctor, was pray. I asked Christ for a miracle for Jonathan and for his father. I didn't do anything else. If what you are saying is true, then Christ answered my prayers, and the prayers of so many others praying for Jonathan. It wasn't me, but it was Jesus who did this."

I go silent after this exchange, and Dr. Charles

also is quiet. Finally, he says, "I'll go find Carol," and then he is gone.

Paula is still there, and she brings a small cup with the mandatory red straw to my bed side. I am again treated to a wonderful sensation as the cold water cools my parched throat. I go back to thinking about what Dr. Charles just told me. "Gone." That word floats in the air around me, and I find myself praying again, but this time it is a prayer of thanksgiving. "Thank you, Lord, for sparing my life, even for a short time longer, and for giving Jonathan his life back. Please Lord. Let it be enough for his father."

The door opens again, and Carol is there. She is as beautiful as ever, but I can see in her eyes the concern of the last few days has drained her. She stands close to the bed, and she takes my right hand into hers.

"Sorry," I offer, knowing all too well it's not nearly enough. A tear runs down her one cheek, and she attempts a smile. "I guess the Lord still wants me to hang in here for a little longer," I offer. Carol shakes her head and then lays her head on my chest, and I can feel her tears falling from her eyes. I put my other hand on her head and pat as she continues to cry softly.

After a few minutes she raises her head back up, and she is looking intensely into my eyes. "Rubin, I just want you to know that I love you. I'm glad to have the chance to tell you that again." I smile at her, not knowing exactly what I look like anymore. I know my head has been shaved bare, and I also sense that I have tubes running out of my head through whatever hat-like covering they have put on my head. I can only imagine what I look like. How could anyone still love the likes of me? But I know what she has said is the truth, and I know another one who sees me even better for who I am, and He, too, loves me.

"Is Laura here too?" I ask, hoping to get to see her as well.

"Yes, she is here too, but you're still in the ICU,

136

and they will not let more than one of us at a time to be with you."

I understand the explanation, but I really do want to see them both at the same time. I know Paula has been listening to everything, staying silent in the background. Almost as if on cue, the door opens again, and I see Dr. Charles coming back in, and with him is my daughter. It is apparent the Doctor has warned both Laura and Carol about what I must look like. Amazingly, I feel no pain, for having had my head cracked open like an egg. I remember looking at Jonathan and seeing the black hue around his eyes, remnants of the blood bruise from the surgery he had undergone as well.

Laura takes in my appearance and does a masterful job of hiding what I know she is likely thinking. "Hi, Dad," she offers. I smile lifting my free hand to her. She moves rapidly to other side of the bed and holds my other hand.

"Tell me about Jonathan?" I ask, wanting to know their impression of what had happened. Laura understands, but looks first at her mom and then at Dr. Charles.

"It's fine," Doctor Charles responds to the unasked question.

Laura looks again at her mother, and I see Carol nod, silently telling Laura to tell the story. Laura begins, "After they took you for the test, Jonathan and his mother started asking questions. Jonathan surprised me, as he asked about Simon the leper first, not Lazarus like I thought he would. He asked, 'Simon told Jesus that if Jesus was willing, he could heal him. Then Jesus said he was willing. If I ask, will Jesus heal me?'

"I explained that we are told to ask, but that not every request gets the type of answer we might be hoping for. I asked him if it would be okay if we prayed for him, and he said yes. Katherine had her hands on his shoulders, and Mom, Sue, and I all put our hands on his

137

shoulders as well, and Mom was praying for him, when he suddenly lost consciousness and slipped out of the chair."

"I think you must already know what they discovered when they got him to the CT Scan room and did the next scan."

I nod, looking at Dr. Charles and saying the single word, "Gone."

We spend the next few minutes reliving that experience, and all three of us are marveling at what has happened.

"They will try and explain away what has happened," Laura offers. I see Dr. Charles stiffen but then nod his head as well.

"Yes, they likely will," he offers. "Jonathan's father had him on quite a cocktail of medicines, trying to kill off the portion of the tumor we had not been able to remove. But the CT scans will clearly show that the drugs had done nothing to kill the tumor, and even the radiation treatments failed to slow the advance of the cancer. It will be difficult not to credit something else as the reason for the sudden cure." But the good doctor sounds anything but convinced.

Dr. Charles looks at Laura and Carol and says, "Rubin needs to rest again, and I am giving him some medication that is going to make that happen. We need to continue to drain off any new blood from the rupture, but I believe we were successful in cutting off the majority of the flow of blood to that portion of the weakened vein, and we were able to reroute another blood flow to the other portion of the vein on the other side of the hemorrhage.

"But as I have told you all, this is at best a temporary fix. If he is going to have any chance at surviving this, he needs to be perfectly still and not engaging in too many other activities like talking."

I watch as he injects something into the bag of fluids that hangs just to the left of my head. I really do

138

not want to sleep any more, as I am too interested in hearing what else has been happening, but within just a couple of minutes the world gets fuzzy, and I am back to being unconscious.

Chapter Fourteen – Nighttime Visitors

When I wake, the room light is muted, but Paula is still there. She sees me open my eyes and comes right over into my line of sight. "Mr. James, are you okay?" she asks.

I think about that for a moment and then say, "Yes, but I am thirsty." Paula reaches over to the collection of items on a shelf and the cup with the red straw appears before me again.

After taking another drink of the cold liquid, Paula is back on the communication device, and I hear her say, "Mr. James is awake again, Doctor."

A few minutes later, Dr. Charles is there.

"What time is it?" I ask.

"It's a little after two in the morning," he says. His smile is warm, and he doesn't look tired, although I suspect he has been sleeping in one of the rooms close to mine. He's been on watch now for four days, and I think Paula has been here all along as well. The doctor confirms my suspicion, as he turns to Paula and says, "Go get some rest. I'll stay with him for the next few hours." Paula does not argue with him, and soon I hear the door close as she leaves.

"The two of you ever sleep?" I ask, attempting to make it sound like a joke.

Dr. Charles just smiles and answers, "Yes, we both do sleep, but this is special, and both Nurse Jones and I are very interested in how you are doing." I guess I look surprised, as I can understand why Dr. Charles is here, but surprised by his deference to the nurse. He continues, "The procedure I did, well it was her idea. She has seen so many of these deep vein aneurisms, in her time working with stroke victims, she came up with the idea, and you were the first patient we ever tried it on. "

141

Suddenly, I am very happy Paula is here as well. "So how am I doing?" I ask.

Dr. Charles just smiles and says, "You're still here." He stops for a moment, and I suspect he is weighing telling me something, and then he continues. "You are actually doing better than I expected. We have been successful in relieving the pressure from the rupture. We have drained off the blood and successfully stopped the bleeding." I am waiting for the "but," but he says no more, just smiles at me.

I feel a wave of hope sweep through me, as if for the first time the imminent death sentence might have been stayed. I think he sees the change in my face, and then tells me the rest of the story.

"Later today, we will be closing up all of the areas we have left open to permit the drains to work. After that you will be able to move a bit, and perhaps we can even move you to a more normal room, where you can have visitors again. You still have a long road ahead of you, and you are doing remarkably well for someone of your age. I guess you are a fighter and have a reason to cling to life. Most patients your age give up."

He is being frank with me. Reminding me I have already had a full life by anyone's standards. And he is right about that and about why I am still clinging to life. I have several reasons but the principal one is that there is a mission I was sent on and it has not been completed.

I hear the door to the room open, and Paula is there again.

"I thought you were going to get some rest," Dr. Charles says. Paula draws him away from the bed and is talking to him in such a low voice I cannot hear what she is telling the doctor, but I do see him nod, whisper something back to her, and then he leaves the room. My curiosity is aroused, and I wonder whether another patient has an emergency need or if he has a call from a

142

family member wondering where he is.

It is pretty amazing how our minds work, as we manufacture answers to questions without knowing exactly what is happening.

Paula is still in my line of sight, and I am about to ask what is happening when the door opens back up, and Dr. Charles is back.

"Thanks, Paula," I hear the doctor say. It's the first time I have heard him refer to her with other than "Nurse Jones." She leaves, and the doctor is back by my bedside.

He looks at me and finally tells me what is going on.

"You have a visitor that is asking to see you," he states.

"At two in the morning?" I say with a bit of surprise.

"I told him I would ask you and that if you say yes, he can only stay for five minutes, as you need your rest to be ready for all that is going to happen later this morning."

"Who is it?" I ask, wondering if Jonathan is here with Kathryn, wanting to talk about what has happened.

Dr. Charles hesitates, but then says, "It's Doctor Baine. He wants to talk with you. You don't have to talk with him now, and I can tell him to go away and come back after you are through with the surgery. But he was insistence that I at least ask."

Jonathan's father is here in the middle of the night. I understand that a part of my mission whether successful or not is about to unfold.

"Yes, I will talk with him."

Dr. Charles nods and then opens the door. He is gone for only a few seconds and returns with Dr. Jeremey Baine following. It does not surprise me, when Dr. Charles takes up a position on the border of my vision. After my last encounter with Jonathan's father, Dr. Charles is in policing action, making sure nothing that is said threatens my physical or mental wellbeing.

143

Everything about Dr. Charles is confirming just how much I like him, and how good of a doctor he really is.

Jeremey looks really out of sorts, and he is obviously struggling to find the words to start. "Thank you for agreeing to see me. I know after our last conversation that you have every right not to want to see me." He stops again, trying to form the words. "I guess, I'm here to say thank you, for whatever it is you did for my son. I certainly didn't deserve it." And then he is weeping and getting down on his knees beside my bed.

"No, don't," I hear myself saying. "I'm not the one responsible for what has happened for Jonathan."

The five minutes Dr. Charles gave Jeremey expands to more than thirty.

The whole discussion is my own "Nicodemus moment." Jeremey had come in the middle of the night to wrestle with what he knows is true but cannot understand. Like Nicodemus he has begun a journey. It would take Nicodemus more than two years, before he would finally declare himself to be a disciple of Jesus by helping Joseph of Arimathea bury the body of Jesus. That road would include his own defense of Jesus, trying to give Jesus a fair hearing before his fellow Pharisees. But it would take Jesus's death before he was willing to risk everything through his actions. I wonder what path Jeremey will now travel.

By the time Jeremey leaves, I realize two of the miracles I had asked for have been granted. I also accept that part of the reason for me still being here, has been completed.

Dr. Charles dims the lights even further after Jeremey is gone. My mind is whirling, considering everything I have told Jeremey, and praying it is enough. I believe the good doctor knows what is going through my mind, and I watch as he once again adds something to the fluid bag beside my bed. I think about objecting, but then know he is doing what he believes is best for

144

me. Even with the additional medicine, I am still awake for some time, and I spend it praying for Jonathan, Kathryn, Jeremey, and myself. There is still one more task to be completed, and I ask for the time to complete that as well.

Chapter Fifteen – Loose Ends

The morning comes much quicker than I expect. I guess being drugged a bit helps with the sense that time is disappearing. Once again, two nurses are pushing my bed, back into the operating theatre. I'm fully awake and see both Dr. Charles and Paula the nurse are gowned up and waiting for me.

Dr. Charles had permitted a brief visit by Carol and by Laura before I was rolled back into surgery. I am happy to see them and realize that both are weathering my constant medical crises as well as can be expected. This time before I am rolled away, both my wife and daughter spend time with me, praying for a successful outcome to the surgery.

Modern medicine is pretty amazing. I guess some of the most significant improvements are with anesthesiology. So much of surgery can now be done without the patient needing to be aware of what is happening. There are times though that even though the patient is sedated, they are still very much aware of what is happening, and it is only after the surgery is complete and the sedating medicines have worn off that the patient is able to explain that they heard everything that was being said and felt much of what was being done. For whatever the reason, this will be one of those times for me. Fortunately, there is no pain, but I am hearing and sensing everything that is happening. It's a bit like having a front row seat watching a play unfolding, where you also happen to be the main character.

To Dr. Charles and Nurse Paula, I appear to be unconscious, but I am hearing everything that is going on. For a portion of the surgery it's like I am watching what is happening from a position just overhead. I do not feel any pain, just sense some of the urgency that is

147

occurring. The first problem occurs when the main drain is removed from the hole left in my skull. Apparently, there is more fluid there than what they expected. I listen as they frantically attempt to figure out where the fluid is coming from, and then having discovered the source, are finally able to stem the flow. The second problem is almost humorous. There is a piece of my skull that they have kept off, and when it is time to find it, to put it back into place, they cannot find it.

Finally, it is discovered, lying on a tray with instruments ready to be tossed out. That brings a few minutes of tension, that Dr. Charles finally breaks by talking about a movie he saw where an emergency surgery is performed on a captain at sea, and the character doing the surgery decides to leave a few marbles from the captain's personal stash inside this particularly annoying captain. The captain discovers the marbles missing from his collection but never figures out where they went. He concludes the story saying, "From that time forward, whenever the crew would refer to the captain as having lost a few marbles or having a few loose marbles, well, they were telling the truth." That story breaks the tension and the sense of trying to discover who is to blame for the misplaced piece of bone. Again, I find myself thinking how blessed I am, to have this doctor working on me.

The surgery takes over three hours to complete, and I gain insights into how these incredibly gifted people work together trying to help me. I find myself thanking the Creator for allowing these folks such insights into how we were designed and put together. I don't know the reason I was given this experience, only that it cements my belief in how much I do not know about myself as a human being.

When I am finally back in the post-surgery recovery room, it takes about twenty minutes for the sedating medicines to wear off for me to communicate.

148

I know it will take hours for the full effects to disappear. Dr. Charles is there waiting for me to emerge from that haze. When I see him, I begin to laugh.

"What's so funny?" he asks.

When I say, "Loose Marbles," at first, he is at a loss, but then makes the connection.

"You heard that?" he asks, his voice noticeably troubled.

I smile, and just say, "It was marvelous. You brought everyone back together with a little laughter, breaking the tension in the room."

He asks a series of other questions, mostly confirming I can still wiggle my toes and fingers, and that I can now turn my head. He asks about pain, and I admit that my backside is sore, probably from being in the same position for so long, but other than that, I am remarkably pain free. He does ask a few more questions, confirming I actually did hear a lot of what was happening. I do not tell him about actually seeing some of it, positioned above the table I was lying on, but I figure that is probably too amazing to bother him with right now.

He leaves, and shortly thereafter, first Carol and then Laura are allowed to visit, only for a few minutes each. After they leave, Dr. Charles is back.

"We are going to keep you here for at least a few hours, monitoring everything. If nothing else comes up, we will move you to a post-surgical room that is a step down from ICU and then tomorrow hopefully to another more normal room. I'm going home, to visit with my family and get some sleep, but the nurses know how to get me, and I will never be more than a half-hour away."

I am amazed he gives me such detail. He could have just left, and I would have never known the difference, but again, he is not like most of the doctors I have experienced in my life. After he leaves, Paula

149

visits briefly and introduces two more nurses from the team. Jackie and Sammy have been tasked with monitoring my progress and the first job is moving me again so my rear stops complaining.

I am also treated to another cold drink, coming from another cup with the red straw. This water is also cold, so it is obvious that Jackie and Sammy have been instructed on my preferred beverage temperature. The room's lights are dimmed so I can sleep if I desire, but I use the time examining everything that has happened and praying again.

When you face life-threatening events, you discover much more about what you really believe, and you learn who you really are. A friend told me, "there are no atheists in fox holes," and I suspect that is also true when you are facing potential life-ending events. I realize now how blessed I am to know there really is a God who is involved in my life.

At one time I thought that if there was a God and if he called all the shots, it would make no sense trying to communicate with Him if what is going to happen is already determined. But that was before I came to grapple with the God who is. While nothing that happens surprises Him, I have also learned that He wants us to talk with him. It is still a bit mysterious to me, but at every turn I have learned that telling Him what is happening and how I am feeling actually is important. I also learned the truth in the statement, "you have not because you have asked not." I learned this as I started to recognize answers to my prayers happening. That doesn't mean I was always getting what I was asking for. I've learned that He is not a slot machine where sometimes you hit the jackpot. I remember a film that made prayer look like a preverbal slot machine. No, instead I started seeing that situations I prayed about would resolve many times far better than I expected.

I've only been in the hospital now a little less

150

than two weeks, and already I have experienced a cornucopia of answered prayers, including two apparent miraculous events. So, I ask again for two things I really am hoping will happen. I know one task that remains to be completed, and I pray I will be given the time to finish that, and I also pray for one other event I would like to be able to witness. There are a ton of other loose ends I pray about as well, so many things that need tending to before my time here is over, but I end my prayer with thanksgiving for everything that has already occurred.

I must have fallen asleep, because it is nurse Jackie who wakes me for the next round of "pokes and prods." Apparently, everything is progressing the way they had hoped. There are several small containers with what looks like Jell-O and apple sauce that have arrived on a tray, and she adjusts the bed, bringing my head and upper part of my body farther up. She opens both containers and then asks if I would like one or the other. I decide on the apple sauce. She hands me the plastic spoon, and I surprise myself by getting most of it into my mouth.

By six in the evening, Jackie and Sammy have discounted some of the electronics and put others in the bed with me. They wheel me out of the ICU and to another room that looks remarkably similar to my first room. I am already looking forward to the next move, to a normal room, and when I ask, it is Sammy who answers, "Tomorrow."

Chapter Sixteen – Tomorrow

I try to sleep but find it impossible. My mind keeps returning to Lazarus's story and wondering what happens next. I also find myself praying about myself and what is in store for me. Every two hours or so either Sammy or Jackie are checking on me, taking measurements, and moving me so I no longer am in danger of bed sores. It is Sammy who informs me that tomorrow, before I get to move to the standard room, I will need to also get out of the bed and try walking a few steps.

I ask her if she could see if there is a Bible around somewhere I could have. She smiles, and says, "I'll be right back." When she returns, she hands me a book I recognize immediately. It's my daughter's "Source Book."

"Your daughter left it with me before she went home last evening. She said you may ask for it. I guess she knows you pretty well!"

"Yes," I answer, and then I add, "And she listens better than anyone I have ever known." Sammy's eyebrows raise a bit, and I know she is trying to understand the comment, but she lets it pass. I find the passage in the Bible, and I read John 11. I spend time looking for every mention of the village of Bethany. I am amazed at the number of individual healings and events that happened there. That gives me plenty to think about and the hours slip by quickly.

The morning is marked by two major undertakings. True to her word, immediately after I eat a little of the breakfast, Sammy and Jackie are both there, and they help me stand for the first time in a while. I am immediately aware of how little strength I have in my legs. They provide both a walker and one of those bottle-carrying, rolling poles I can hang on to. They also have a wheelchair brought to my room. I am determined to try and walk a little, and I head to the bathroom for

153

the other feat I want to accomplish. Sammy immediately understands where I am headed. Amazingly, she helps me there, and helps me get seated on the toilet that is equipped with a raised toilet seat, so I don't sit nearly as low. Whoever came up with the idea for these cushioned, raised toilet seats deserves a medal! They even give me a few minutes of privacy, and I believe they can hear me celebrating not needing to use the bed pan again. You never realize how marvelous the little things are in life, until you are unable to do some of these most basic activities.

Jackie is the one who helps me stand up from my bathroom activities, as I am still wobbling. But she looks at me and smiles. It's then for the first time I get to see myself in the mirror and stop. I don't recognize the person staring back at me. I've always been a bit pudgy, and my round face always seemed to fit the rest of me. I also have always been meticulous about shaving. The image in the mirror has a colored beanie cap on, covering an obviously bald head, but the face is no longer rounded, and there is stubble growing around my chin. The brown eyes seemed to have grown in proportion to the face, and there are patches almost like bruises on my cheeks and under my eyes.

Jackie sees me staring and says, "You already look better than you did just yesterday." I wonder how that is even possible. Then I remember how close to death I had come. Jackie helps me back to my bed, and I am glad to be prone again.

"I'll let you rest a little, and then we are taking you for another CAT scan, just to check on how things are progressing. After that, if everything is okay, we will move you to your new room," Jackie offers.

Two other nurses arrive, and I recognize one from my first conscious visit to the scanner. Rose smiles at me when she realizes I remember her. "How you doing, Mr. James?" Rose asks. They are already pushing my bed out of the room with Jackie holding the door. I am

154

still a little at a loss for words, with my mirror image still floating in my mind.

I finally manage, "I guess I am okay," and I go back to thinking about that image.

When we get to the CAT scan room, Mildred is not there. Instead it is a younger man operating the scanner this morning. His badge says his name is Martin Mitchell, and while he is efficient, he doesn't have the friendly attitude of Mildred. He does relay the information about the music, the clunking, and the lights, so I realize there are some standard protocols that come with the job. I spend my thirty minutes in the tube praying. I guess that mirror image really struck home, and I am asking for the strength to accept what I saw.

The scan is finally done, and Rose and the other nurse are there to wheel me back upstairs. Rose seems to sense something is bothering me, and she asks the same question again. "How are you doing, Mr. James?"

At that same moment I am thinking about Jonathan's observation the first time we met on the way to this same scanning experience. His "you're old" has new meaning for me. "I'm old and I'm ugly," I state, answering her question. Rose is a bit taken back by that, as I have a reputation of being a generally pleasant patient.

Her response snaps me out of my funk. "Na, you're not ugly, just old!" I cannot help myself as I start laughing and tearing up at the same time.

The Lord's providence never ceases to amaze me. It was the perfect answer to my wallowing in self-pity. I'm still chuckling as they roll me into my room, but it is not the room I thought I was going back to, instead this room is one floor below the area I came from. This room is, how do I say it? Palatial, with two couches, at least eight high-back reclining chairs, several large flatscreen devices hanging on the walls, and whole bank of equipment positioned around the room. In the room are already almost a dozen people. My wife, daughter, my

155

friend Louis, aka The Stork, Jonathan Baine with both Kathrine and Jeremey his parents, and Dr. Charles with three of my nurses is there as well. With Rose and the nurse I have not identified yet, there are an even dozen people there. As soon as they position my bed, Dr. Charles says, "Rubin, welcome to the prime ministers' suite!" and then there is clapping occurring all around me,

I am confused and delighted at the same time, and another of my prayers is about to be answered. I see my daughter is holding the bundle of papers, and she is already organizing them to get back to where we had left off the story. Jackie, one of the nurses, hands Laura back her Bible, which they had given me last night. Dr. Charles continues, "The hospital reserves this room for very important people. It has housed the likes of Winston Churchill when he came here with his heart condition, and even has seen the queen and some of the other royals when they needed treatments. It turns out it's the only room in the hospital where this many people can visit at the same time! And fortunately, it has not been used for over a year, and you get to use it!"

Even as Dr. Charles finishes his brief explanation, the door opens again, and Mildred is there with the young man from the CAT Scanning room. I had been so self- absorbed in my own worries, I had not made the connection. But seeing Mildred and Martin together, I see the family resemblance. But what is even more surprising is when Dr. Charles walks over to Mildred and puts his arm around her shoulders. I look at Martin and suddenly it all comes together. Martin is their son.

Dr. Charles sees my surprise, and smiling says, "Mildred and I thought it best that she uses her maiden name when working here. It was hard enough getting me a position here when she was already such a fixture in the hospital. We met here when I was a resident and she already was the master for the new scanning wing of the hospital."

156

"But enough about me, we all came here because this story your daughter is reading has already caused quite a stir, and frankly we better get back to it. If you think it was hard getting you this room, you have to imagine what it was like coordinating all of these people's time off so they could be here!"

Everyone looks for a place to sit. When it begins, it looks a bit like the game musical chairs, but there are more than enough places, and now fourteen people are seated, with Laura sitting on the chair closest to where my bed is positioned. She has turned the chair, so she is facing away from me and toward everyone else. I'm watching Jeremy Baine, because despite our late-evening visit and talk, I suspect he probably has the most questions of anyone in the room. But he is being attentive to his wife and to his son. Jonathan looks amazing. In the three days since I last saw him, he has already begun to fill out his almost skeleton-like form, and he is no longer wearing his beanie cap and a dusting of black hair is already beginning to cover his former baldness. But what is most impressive are his eyes. They flash with almost the same intensity as my daughter's.

Laura looks back at me to see if I am ready, and I nod. It is only a few seconds and she is back into the story.

Chapter Seventeen – Aftermath

I am often asked about what my first impressions were after I had been freed from the grave wrappings. Fortunately, Cain had an additional cloak with him, as I had not been wrapped with clothing on. So, I was spared the additional embarrassment of needing to walk back to my house naked. But the first thing I wanted to do was to bathe. The scent of the spices and perfumes was overwhelming, but it was the memory of that rotting smell that made me seek refuge in our side room while my sisters brought me water to allow me to wash my body.

Jesus, his disciples, the crowd that followed him, and all our neighbors and friends stood outside our house, and there was a mixture of singing, questioning, and praising God going on. Later, I would learn that some of the people who had witnessed my coming forth from the grave went to the Pharisees and later to the great council in Jerusalem and reported what had happened. Instead of wonderment, most of the leaders responded in fear and resentment.

One of the men even asked, "What are we doing? For this man is performing many signs. If we let Him go on like this, all men will believe in Him, and the Romans will come and both take away our place and our nation."

In hindsight it was the truest revelation of what was really driving our leaders. They valued their positions as leaders, they envied the power revealed in the various miracles Jesus was displaying, and they feared the Roman reaction to the people embracing Jesus as something more than a traveling preacher. The planning for capturing and doing away with Jesus entered a fevered pitch after Jesus raised me from the dead. They also decided that my life, too, must be forfeited, as news of my return from the dead was too much evidence to hide. That fact would lead my sisters

159

and I to make a decision that would send me away from Bethany for the rest of my life, and to this island that would become my home.

It was a strange time, for the very signs they saw pointing to who Jesus really was were driving them to destroy what our people had been looking forward to for generations. They knew the promises, but instead of rejoicing in the fulfillment of the prophecies, they willingly chose to destroy the miracle worker, not realizing that in so doing they were fulfilling the greatest of the promises.

Nicodemus was present for these discussions and relayed the comments to us after Jesus had been killed. Everything was moving quickly now. It was only a couple of weeks before the third Passover would occur since Jesus had started his ministry. All the leaders were seeking Jesus, to seize him, yet they feared doing it openly for fear of how the people would respond.

Those weeks before Passover were filled with activity for my family as well. Everyone wanted to see Jesus, and everyone wanted to see me. Six days before the Passover celebration began, Jesus returned to Bethany. Simon the Leper, whom Jesus had healed earlier, had the largest house in Bethany. He had asked Martha about helping him prepare and host a dinner for Jesus and his closest disciples. Martha was overjoyed with the idea, and both I and Mary were invited. Simon's home included a very large and spacious room where the dinner could be held, that would easily hold over fifty people.

I knew something was bothering my sister Mary. Ever since I had returned home, she had been quiet. While Martha had been bubbling with excitement, Mary had stayed withdrawn as if in contemplation. While both of my sisters were impacted by my death, the experience for Mary was far worse than for Martha. Even though both my sisters had used practically the same words when they met Jesus before he called me back to life,

160

Mary's grief and feeling of betrayal was deeper.

I was grateful Simon had also invited Cain to the meal. I knew Cain was still unaware of Mary's love for him and that she was still waiting for Cain to admit how he felt about her. But at least Cain would be there for her. But it was at the meal that the full extent of Mary's understanding of who Jesus was and what was about to happen was put on full display for all of us.

Martha had already helped others serve the main portion of the meal when Mary arrived in the room carrying a large vial of one of our most costly perfumes. Nard is used in many of our rituals, and it is also one of the ointments used in preparing a person for burial. It is very fragrant, and even a little amount can fill a room with its aroma. She approached Jesus and the room fell strangely quiet, with the many conversations suddenly stopping and everyone watching her approach, unsure of what she intended. I was there, reclining just a few cushions away from where Jesus was reclining.

Mary first opened the vial and poured some of the perfume on Jesus's head, and then she knelt before Jesus, loosened her hair, which reached her waist, and poured the Nard over Jesus's feet. She then bent even lower and using her hair wiped Jesus's feet. The fragrance of the Nard filled the room immediately, and she had used a great deal of the ointment, so the potency of the fragrance continued to grow. What Mary did brought gasps from many in the room. Mary was displaying an affection for Jesus beyond anything I had witnessed before. One of Jesus's disciples broke the trance-like atmosphere when he said, "Why was this perfume not sold for three hundred denarii and given to poor people?"

That disciple had correctly identified the value of that perfume. That one vial would have brought almost the equivalent of an entire year's wages for the average worker in Bethany. I was surprised by this display of affection but strangely moved by it at the same time.

161

Others at the meal picked up on the comment made by the disciple echoing the sentiment. But Jesus silenced the room as he said, "Let her alone, why do you bother her? She has done a good deed to Me. For you always have the poor with you, and whenever you wish you can do good to them, but you do not always have Me. She has done what she could; she has anointed My body beforehand for the burial. Truly I say to you, whenever the gospel is preached in the whole world, what this woman has done will also be spoken of in memory of her."

Jesus took Mary's hand and raised her up from her knees. Mary left the room quickly, and I got up and followed her as well. I found Mary in another room, and she was with Cain who was holding her. She was weeping, and Cain was trying to comfort her. The fragrance of the perfume swirled around us. When Cain saw me enter, he tried to free Mary from his embrace, but she would not release him.

She finally turned to me, and before I could ask, she said, "He is going to die," and she continued her sobbing.

It was that event that finally broke down the walls that had prevented Cain and Mary from ever confronting their feelings for each other. It was at the point of greatest sorrow, that Cain's love for Mary finally was displayed in his caring for her, and it was in that caring Cain discovered Mary had been his since he had faced down those ruffians so many years ago. It was also at that moment, I understood Mary had been given an understanding of who Jesus was, and what his mission would cost, far beyond what any of us really understood at this point.

I would learn later that it was Jesus's rebuke of the disciple who had started the whispering about Mary's extravagant use of the perfume that cemented his decision to betray Jesus to our leaders. It was also the start of the most amazing week in my own history and I

162

believe the history of this world. For the next day Jesus would be hailed as the coming Messiah by the people in our great city, and then six days later the same people would cry out for his death.

Laura stops reading, and the room is quiet, waiting for what is next. The stack of sheets she has left to read has shrunk considerably. But it is Jonathan who breaks the silence. "I don't understand, if Jesus has done all these miracles, raising Lazarus from death, why would the leaders want to kill him and Lazarus? And how did Mary know that Jesus was going to die?" Leave it to the child to open the door to the heart of the story.

Laura is looking at me, and I know she wants me to begin to answer the questions. The task I was prepared for is now before me. I begin with my own story, explaining how the miraculous had driven me to want to destroy the evidence of the truth. As I finish my story, I end with, "So I understand why despite the miracles, the leaders wanted to kill Jesus. When you come face to face with God, our response is not one of acceptance or even gratefulness, but it is one of fear and anger. God needs to do something in us before we will respond positively to His call."

It is Jeremey who asks the most difficult of the questions. "If God needs to do something in us, before we respond to his call, why doesn't He do that change for everyone when they are born or even before they are born? Why bring anyone into existence without also changing them so they will respond to His call? And why wait until they are older when the person has already spent so much of their life running after other things?"

His words were not hostile but filled with real wonderment. The tone answered for me one of my concerns, Jeremey was no longer fighting against God; he was now at the point of asking, "Why me?" That is the question that still flares up within my own soul, and it is difficult to accept the answer I now know is true,

163

"Because He loved me first, before I came to love him."

I ask Laura, "May I use your Bible?"

She puts the sheets yet to be read beside her and then stands, bringing her Bible to me. I accept it, and then press the up button on my bed so the upper part of me is once again raised to make it easier for me to read. I turn to Romans 5:8 and read that verse first. Starting from there I explain what has become my own good news. That Jesus loved me, died for me, and then insured that I would come to see and accept that love. "I cannot explain why Jesus loves me, as when I look at my life I see nothing in it that would attract anyone to me, but I am grateful He does love me, and that He chose me to be counted as one of His friends. "

Jeremey's head is nodding, and I am grateful that something I have said, is connecting with him. I look over at Jonathan and then answer his question about Mary. "Jonathan, you asked how Mary knew Jesus was going to die? I believe there are two answers to that question. First off, even the leaders knew of the prophecies pointing to a suffering Messiah. I turn to Isaiah 53 and read the entire chapter. "You see Mary knew this prophecy about the Messiah, and she made the connection between Jesus being the Messiah and this prophecy. But I believe she also was granted an understanding even greater. After suffering the death of her brother, and seeing him being returned to life, she knows the miracle points to the only power that could overcome death itself, and for that power to be fully manifested, it meant Jesus would need to shatter the chains of death. The words she heard Jesus speak, she understood better than the other people present, and even her anointing of Jesus came from that conviction in her heart, of who He was and what He was about to do."

The door to this palatial suite opens, and I turn to see another nurse carrying a file enter the room. Seeing Dr. Charles, she says, "Sorry, everyone. Dr. Charles, can I talk with you?" Dr. Charles stands and walks to the

164

nurse and then out the door. After the door closes different conversations start among the people gathered there. I am grateful that none of the conversations are directed at me, and I close my eyes, praying silently. My thoughts were a bit of a jumble, but I give thanks for the words I was given and pray that those words might bring Jesus honor.

Dr. Charles is back after about ten minutes.

"Folks, it is almost lunch time, and I have asked Jennifer," he points to the nurse who had just interrupted us, "to take you all to the cafeteria here to grab a bite to eat. We can all come back after lunch, and that will give Rubin, Carol, and Laura some time as well to eat their own lunch."

"That's a great idea, I'm starved!" Jonathan states. Everyone laughs at that pronouncement, as it is obvious to us all that something dramatic has changed in his life. Nourishment means something different for him now. I cannot help but chuckle as well, recalling the gaunt image of him that still such a recent memory. Everyone is standing, and they are all making for the door and following Jennifer out of the room. I look at Dr. Charles and realize there is another reason he has set up a method to get everyone else out of the room. I look at my wife and Laura and know they are thinking the same thing.

Once everyone is out of the room and the door is closed, Dr. Charles sits down on one of the chairs. He is looking at me, and I am waiting for him to tell us all what is going on.

"Rubin", he starts and then stops. He finally composes himself enough that he can speak.

"Rubin, the CAT scan shows another problem and it is not good news."

For the next ten minutes Dr. Charles explains the situation. I look at Carol and realize she is actually accepting the news better than what I would expect. Even Laura is no longer devasted by the explanation.

165

Both look at me. I look back at Dr. Charles, who seems to be the most upset of us.

Carol asks, "Rubin, what do you want to do?"

I smile at both my wife and my daughter and then answer, "I would like to go home."

Chapter Eighteen – Going Home

Dr. Charles stays with us through lunch. His plate is untouched when the folks who pick up the trays return to the room. My wife and daughter have picked at their food, eating practically nothing. I, on the other hand, am hungry, and I eat a surprising amount of the applesauce and a good portion of the chicken, rice, and string beans that were on the plate delivered to me.

After our plates are removed, it is my wife who asks, "What are you going to tell everyone when they get back?"

I have been thinking about and praying for the answer to that question. I offer up an answer: "I think I want to see what questions they may still have from this morning, but then see if we cannot get back into having Laura read the rest of the testimony. Then after that is done, we will see whether I am ready to tell them what is happening." I look at Carol and then Laura and see they are okay with this plan. Even Dr. Charles looks relieved that I don't want to just jump right into my own news.

It's one-thirty when everyone gets back. I hear Jonathan in the hall even before the door opens. His voice is upbeat and strong, a far cry from where he had been just a few short days ago. Jonathan is still laughing when the door opens. Unlike the first time, everyone knows where their seats are, and they quickly resume their positions.

"Do you have any more questions about the sections we read this morning?" I ask.

It's Kathryn who responds for the group. "We talked a lot at lunch, and while we do have more questions, we want to hear the rest of the story. Jeremey and I need to take Jonathan home by four, and we all wanted to hear the outcome of the story, if that is okay? That way we can continue with our questions tomorrow."

167

I look around the room, and I am relieved to see everyone agrees with Katherine's recommendation. I turn to Laura who is already shuffling the papers on her lap and seems ready to begin. She jumps right into the story, without preamble or any questions. I know she is still processing the news, and right now she just wants to finish the story so she can process everything without having the need to finish the story still hanging over her.

The next morning came quickly, and the throngs of people who were entering the city for the festival were even more excited to know Jesus was coming as well. Everyone had to pass through Bethany to make that final journey up the incline and through both the Mount of Olives and the final winding path into the city. Some of the people who had seen Jesus call me from the grave were telling of that event to anyone who wanted to listen. Jesus's disciples found a young donkey, and they put a cloak on it. Jesus made the ascent from Bethany to Jerusalem riding on that animal. The fragrance of the perfume that had poured on Jesus still was present. All the people were waving the branches of palm trees before him and shouting "Hosanna! Blessed is he who comes in the name of the Lord, even the King of Israel."

It was no wonder our leaders were saying everything they had done so far was not doing any good. One even exclaimed, "The world has gone after him!"

Martha, Mary, and I stayed in Bethany, watching Jesus beginning this journey. Mary and Martha would see him again. Martha often followed Jesus more closely than either Mary or I did. Normally, at least, Martha would have been there in the crowd, but when she heard of the threats against my life, she stayed with us.

My friend Nathan had found us late the evening before, after Mary had anointed Jesus, and relayed what he had heard in the city. "They are looking for you, Lazarus. They want to kill you as well." Together my sisters and Nathan convinced me that I need to hide myself. Even now, men sent from the leaders were

168

examining all of the crowd following Jesus into Jerusalem. Nathan offered to let me stay at his home, and both my sisters agreed.

So, for the next five days, I was hidden away, waiting for news in my friend's home. Martha visited me twice during this time, always with the news she heard from the city. She even brought news that men had come to our home, seeking me, but had discovered I was not there. They left my sisters alone, but it was clear that Nathan's warning and offer probably had saved my life.

It was Mary who came to me on the day before the Sabbath when the sky had turned black with the news that Jesus had been killed by the Romans, crucified with two other criminals. That news stunned me. How was that possible, that the people would allow the Romans to kill him?

But it was Martha who filled in the rest of the story, as she had been in the crowd and had heard many of our own people crying out for his death. Later, after Jesus had risen, we would learn of Joseph and Nicodemus and their role in burying Jesus. It was Martha and Mary who gave the other women who were following Jesus the spices and ointments they would need to complete his burial. There had been no time to do that before he had been laid in the tomb, because of the closeness of the Sabbath. Early on the morning after the Sabbath, those women had gone to the tomb, hoping to complete what had been left undone. It was they who were the first to meet Jesus after he had arisen from death.

I would not see Jesus again in this life. But I had no doubts about what others would tell me, about having seen him after his death. I already knew and believed my friend, the carpenter's son, was the promised one.

On that Sabbath day, Nathan had rushed into his home, and told me, "They know you are here, and they are coming to seize you." My sisters and I had prepared for this potential. We had already agreed I would leave

169

Nathan's house and make my way to this island where our family already had contacts with a few merchants. Some of our spices came from vendors there. Nathan had prepared much of what I would need. I would learn later that my departure missed those searching for me by less than an hour.

The journey would take almost three months. I was accepted into the community on the island known as Cyprus, but even at this great distance, word of what was happening would reach me often. Before I left, Cain had requested the permission to wed Mary. I gladly gave my permission two days before Jesus was put to death. Mary and Cain would travel with Joseph of Arimathea, the man whose tomb Jesus had been laid in. Together they would arrive in Gaul before crossing over to Britannia. Like Jesus, I, too, would not see Cain or Mary again, but I heard the stories of the man with the flashing green eyes who spoke of Jesus and the miracle of sight he had been given.

When Ruth and Caleb arrived here on this island, they also brought news about my sister Martha. Martha had continued on in Bethany, even after Mary and Cain had left with Joseph. She had made sure each of the families who had worked with us for so many years, gained title to their groves and vineyards. She stayed close to John and was often found in the company of Mary the mother of Jesus, and Mary Magdalene, one of the women to first see Jesus alive after his death. When Mary, the mother of Jesus, departed this life, Martha followed John and supported him with the resources our family had gathered. She would visit me twice on the island. Once when she learned I had asked Ruth to be my wife, and then one final time when she learned Mary had been killed by the Romans in Britannia.

Shortly after Ruth became my wife, Paul and Barnabas arrived on the island and sought me out. By then almost any who had ears knew of my teaching on Jesus and knew of the miracle I had experienced. Paul

170

told me his story, and I marveled at the miracle that would change such an adversary into such a witness for the truth of Jesus. Even before he arrived, I had heard of this man who had a way with words and would fearlessly lay out the case from our scriptures for Jesus being the promised Messiah. He was a stocky man, not large of stature, but his ability at tying together all the various portions of scripture that spoke of the Messiah was amazing.

I called together the people who had listened to my story and who now came to me regularly to hear more about Jesus. That first Sabbath Paul was here, he taught about Jesus and why Jesus had died, and why it was necessary that Jesus physically be raised. He spoke of the miracle I had experienced as the foreshadow of the far greater miracle of Jesus's own resurrection. After his preaching, even more people identified as believers in and followers of Jesus.

Barnabas was the quieter one, but I learned immediately why he was called "the encourager." It was he who explained how the disciples in Jerusalem had started to organize the local gatherings of people and how elders would teach and guide the gatherings while deacons took care of the physical needs of everyone in the body. They learned of my care for the widows and orphans on the island, and it was Barnabas who commended that activity and asked if I would shepherd the people who were coming to believe in Jesus. Before they left, they laid hands on me and charged me with the care of the flock on the island. I would never see either man again, although travelers would often speak of where they had been seen or heard. Paul's letters would arrive by those travelers, and we would read them together at the fellowship meetings. They brought lively discussion and caused us to often reexamine some of the scriptures in the light of those letters.

The years would pass by quickly. Our fellowship continued to grow. I still mixed spices and ointments

171

and used the money our family business had made to help as many as we could on the island. Ruth and I would often be found in the evenings walking along the water line. The beach is mostly stony, but there were areas where the sand was soft and stone free, and it was there we would often sit and relive so many different events we had experienced. We had no children, not that we had not tried, but after ten years, we accepted that the Lord had determined we would not have that blessing. Instead we brought several orphans into our household, and after a number of years we had the blessing of children calling us father and mother.

Those children are all grown now, and most have their own families. They still visit with me from time to time, and we relive together the good days of our lives and talk of what Jesus had done both for me and for their mother. We would talk about what he was still doing in each of their lives.

Ruth would die nineteen years after Paul and Barnabas's visit. It would be while attending to the needs of some of the widows who were sick, that Ruth, too, became sick. For days I cared for her, prayed with her, and used the various ointments and spices that made up what I knew medicinally might help. It was a heart-wrenching time, to watch this woman who had so perfectly understood me and my experience slowly slip away. The evening before she would die for the second time, I carried her out to the water in the early evening, and just held her. I watched as she scanned the water line, watching the birds that floated on the breeze, and her smile was reward enough. Her "thank you" just added to my heart's sorrow, as I knew this was likely the last time she would relish the beauty of the water.

On the last day, she awoke, incredibly weak, but called to me. I sat beside her and picked her up, cuddling her in my lap. She looked at me and said, "Lazarus, I'm going back home, so you need to release me." Even now amid her second great struggle she knew my own leaning even better than I did. "I'll finally be whole. I will see you soon. I love you." Those were her last words to me. She died in my arms.

I buried her in a little crypt I had bought, and I have directed the fellowship to bury me there with her. So now you know my story. But there is one final detail I will leave you with. You see when Ruth told me "I'll finally be whole" I knew exactly what she was talking about. You see, she and I both had seen the other side. When we saw those people we knew, who had gone before us, while they were like us, there was something radically different.

Jesus had changed all of us, but these ones who had died and were not called back to this life were also completely free of any shadow. They were bright spirits waiting for that joining back with what will be their perfect bodies. They are forever free from sin, and both Ruth and I, well, we returned alive but still not freed totally from sin. That is why it was necessary for Ruth to die, and why I, too, must die again. Being whole means finally to have sin conquered once and for all. That is what Ruth wanted, and that is what I want as well. But I will tell you a mystery. Paul talks of it in one of his letters. There are some who will not die but who will experience that changing in the twinkling of an eye, when Jesus returns and brings with him all those whom he loves, and who will live with him. It is my hope that perhaps my life's story might draw you to Jesus. He is the only one who can make you whole.

Laura's voice falters for a moment, and then she continues, but in a different voice.

This testimony was given to me by Lazarus. After he died, I journeyed, as he had directed, and found the son of Cain, the blind man given eyes by Jesus, and Mary his sister. Both Cain and Mary had been put to death by the Romans, but their son had collected several testimonies of others who had experienced healings by Jesus, and this testimony is being given to him as well.

173

When I return home, I will complete the final request Lazarus made of me. He asked that his tomb be marked with this statement, "Lazarus, four days dead, a friend of Christ."

Laura stops talking, slowly turning the final page onto the pile of papers beside her. No one is saying anything. After a few minutes of silence, it is Kathryn who states, "His story is so sad, that he had to lose his wife and then that he had to die again as well."

It is Jonathan, her son, who responds to his mother's comment. "Yes, Mom, it's sad, but his words are also filled with hope. He isn't despairing that he is dying again. Instead he has something to look forward to. That's what is so amazing, Jesus has given him hope. Just like Jesus has given me hope." Leave it to the child to sum up the story.

I watch as Jeremey and Kathryn both appraise their son, and then smile at him. It is obvious they are both amazed and proud at their son's response. I know the time is right, and I say softly, "Yes and Jesus has given me hope as well, because I, too, must go to be whole as well."

Jonathan understands the words faster than anyone else in the room. "But I thought the operation saved you?" he states, in a voice quivering with emotion. The room is silent again, waiting for my comment and his to be explained.

"The operation did what no one expected. It stopped me from dying instantly from that blood vein bursting. But it only gave me some more time; it did not change the fact that I am dying. I wanted to be here, to share in the telling of Lazarus's story, and to hear it all for myself as well. And I am grateful I was given that opportunity. But it is time for me to also go home. But like Lazarus I, too, have hope."

"When are you going to die?" Jonathan's words again ask, soft but close to tears.

"Jonathan, I don't know, but soon. I am going

174

back to my home with my wife and Laura today, and I want to see that home again and be with them for whatever time I have left. But as you said, 'I'm old' and I have had an amazing life. Jesus saved me, and I know He loves me, so this isn't goodbye, it just until we meet again."

My words do seem to comfort him a bit, but I see many eyes in the room have teared up. Jonathan stands and walks over to my bed. He lays his head on my lap and closes his eyes with tears leaking out of them. He asks a final question so softly only I can hear it.

"Why me and not you?"

I stroke his head gently and whisper, "Because He still has tasks for you to complete, but mine are finally done."

Epilogue – A Wedding Foretold

It is a remarkably beautiful day for the fall in England. This country is noted for the seemingly endless mist and rain that so often marks so much of the year. That is why everything is so green here. Being an island surrounded by water, we really should not be surprised at our soggy weather, but today is going to be different, and I am grateful God has provided us with such a beautiful day.

It's been fifteen years since I promised Rubin, two days before he did finally die, that I would fulfill this wish. How he knew this event would happen is beyond my ability to even speculate. That he would ask me to fulfill this wish after all the grief I caused him still surprises me, but Rubin always was full of surprises. He had survived that guaranteed-death event, although my colleague Dr. Charles and his nurse associate, Paula Jones, had pioneered a new surgery procedure that has now saved countless lives, but Rubin was the first. Even after the aftermath of the surgery brought on other issues that would finally take his life, he beat out the estimate of a few days maybe a week, by more than a month.

And nurse Paula Jones is now Dr. Paula Jones. After Dr. Charles explained her role in developing the new treatment, her application for medical school flew through the red tape. Within three years she was back, working alongside Dr. Charles as a full partner in his practice.

Rubin's dearest friend, Dr. Louis Benton, "The Stork," followed him into death less than a month after he died. It was like Rubin's death had removed one of the underpinnings that kept "The Stork" going. But before he died, Dr. Louis accepted Christ as his savior as well.

But the other thirteen people in that gathering are still alive and well, and that gathering has grown into a fellowship now of over five-hundred families just in our

177

community. Our hospital culture has changed remarkably, and two years ago the doctors and nurses did something unheard of; they bought the hospital from the corporation that ran it, and we changed its name to "The Rubin James Christian Hospital." We are noted for taking in the hopeless cases, and several endowments have insured that everyone gets treated the same, whether they can afford to pay or not. Dr. Charles Birmingham leads the board that oversees the hospital, and I still work there, continuing the same work I have done now for nearly forty years.

For a country marked by a general decline in religious faith, our congregation has grown remarkably large, and already has spawned three sister fellowships in other parts of England. Since so many of us are in the medical field, I guess it is not surprising that three more hospitals are being impacted by our members. The fellowship is marked by a belief in the Bible, and in a belief in the miracles described in the Bible that point to who Jesus is. Those stories are repeated often in our gatherings, and the importance of each and the impact on the lives of the individuals are discussed in detail. That belief has changed how we view each patient who comes under our care, and many patients are surprised by our desire to pray with and for them.

As for Rubin's wife, Carol also is involved in our hospital. We have so many foreigners who do not speak English now in our country. She leads a group of linguists who use their gifts to help explain what the problems are the people are experiencing and then also explain the treatments the doctors and nurses are performing. What was primarily an academic gift has turned into a very practical one as well. What is particularly exciting is so many of our patients have never heard of Jesus, and they are intrigued by the general friendliness and care of the staff. It is not unusual to hear one of the linguists translate a patient's question and say, "She wants to know why you are

178

always so happy and friendly?" Or even more often "Why do you have such hope for me; everyone else has given up on me?" It is easy for me to identify the name of Jesus, and I know another person is being exposed to the good news of who Jesus is.

That doesn't mean there are never times of trouble or concern. When Jonathan came to us and told both me and his mother where he wanted to go to school after he finished his undergrad work, I was really upset. He had always indicated he wanted to be a doctor like me, and I had planned out his career ending up with him working beside me. It took me a while to accept his "Dad, I want to be a doctor of souls" as an acceptable substitute. He finally got through to me when he pointed to what Jesus had said to Peter and Andrew when they left their father's fishing business and said, "You will be fishers of men."

Jonathan graduated his program with honors, and last week he was ordained as a minister, and has already accepted a call to a fellowship. It is going to be an experience for me, knowing I and his mother will now be sitting under his preaching. But I heard his first sermon as part of his interview process, and it was amazing. He has fallen totally in love with Jesus, and his desire is that everyone he talks to will also. And one of my prayers was answered. I had been afraid he would accept one of the many invitations that had been sent to him to pastor so many other churches. Even churches in the United States had heard him speak, and everyone wanted him to consider their congregation. I don't know how long he will stay with our fellowship, as some of these other fellowships already number in the thousands. But I am grateful he has chosen to stay here for the time being.

The scars of his cancer are hidden now by his wavy sandy-colored hair. Before his surgery, his hair had been straight and jet black, like mine. But something changed in his chemistry. That wasn't unheard of, as the

179

trauma could cause significant changes to the cells producing the hair. I was just glad he had hair and looked normal, but he has changed. And so have I.

It would take me over two years to come to terms with what had happened, and to finally accept what I knew was true. I can't explain why some people hear the story of Jesus and believe right away, and others of us, like me, take years before they finally yield to the hound of heaven. It took a miracle for Jonathan to start me on that path, and then more than a year after Rubin had died, for me to stand and acknowledge the other miracle that brought me to Jesus.

I saw Rubin a dozen times after he returned home. He was always gentle with me, never pushing me, and always answering my questions with patience. The hope he shone with drew me closer to the One who had changed his life. The day before he died, both Jonathan and I visited Rubin. Jonathan had brought the pouch with the coin, that emblem of hope, back to give it to Rubin. When we left, that pouch and coin were around my neck and hidden under my shirt. I cannot tell you how many times I have touched that pouch and thanked the Lord for a friend like Rubin.

And that brings me to today and Laura James. She has always been unique. Her linguistic gifts have become well known in the academic world. She has amassed several doctorates already and has consulted with many of the archaeological experts who continue to unearth written documents in so many ancient languages. Her abilities have astounded many in the academic world. She has already published several scholarly works and her latest book on another group of scrolls discovered close to the Dead Sea Scrolls area is causing quite a storm of discussion.

She still tints her hair, but instead of the purple coloring of her youth, her dark brown hair has a streak of reddish-blonde that now reaches past her waist and accents her beauty to an amazing level. She has grown

180

out of the many piercings she had as a youngster, but she still wears long and ornate earrings. But her green eyes still flash with an intensity that unnerves many people when they first meet her.

Rubin knew he would not live to see this day. His request of me was that I would walk Laura down the aisle on the day of her wedding. Today is that day. For being such a non-traditionalist as a youth, I am amazed she has worked with her mother to make her wedding so incredibly traditional.

To say I am nervous would be an understatement. I still cannot believe she is marrying the man she is. Rubin had been right on that insight as well. I have told her soon-to-be husband how incredibly fortunate he is to have a woman of this caliber falling in love with him. His words to me explaining his agreement are simple, "I fell in love with her the first time I saw her, and I knew she would be the only woman I would ever love."

I accept his statement as being true. I watched their long courtship, beginning after he graduated from his college. She was still eight years older than he was, but the age difference did not seem to bother either of them.

I see her emerge from her dressing room, the long flowing white gown perfectly sculpted to her figure. There is no doubt she is startlingly beautiful. She takes my offered arm and whispers, "Thank you for doing this. My father told me he had asked you to do this before he died. I know how important it was to him that you be the one to stand in for him."

I look at her eyes that are ablaze with life, and all can say is, "It is my honor."

Together we walk to the church doors and the white runner that runs all the way to the front. Her mother, Carol, is already seated in the first row, and the church is packed with over five-hundred people in attendance. I see my wife, Kathryn, looking back at me. She has a tissue in her hand, and I know there will be

181

tears, but these will be tears of joy.

The pastor is at the front, as are the groom and his selected ushers and best man. Laura's bridal attendants have already made their entrance, and all that is left is for me to walk Laura down the aisle. The music starts, and I feel my knees being sort of wobbly when we start down the aisle, but somehow, I hold it together. I imagine Rubin is watching us and smiling from the great distance that separates us at this point. Yet, I feel like he is right there as well.

We transverse the distance in just a few seconds, but it is at the end that my knees almost do fail me. But finally, I am taking Laura's hand and placing it in the outstretched hand of her soon-to-be husband, my son, Jonathan.

A Peek At Book Three In The Miracles Of Christ Series

Eyewitness – The Saints Released

The herders would tell the story of this day for many years. All I could do is watch in amazement as the massive group of animals ran shrieking down the hill toward the water. I understood their flight and their screaming. After all, I had sounded like them for so many years. The voices in my mind had often taken control of my actions and thrown me against the rocks and at other times into bushes filled with needles, all in order to inflict as much pain as possible. I was always present, always aware of what was being done, and always feeling all of the agony being inflicted upon me, but I was helpless against the powers that controlled me.

It had not always been that way. I still remember the first time I heard the voice. That voice told me that what I desired was my right. After all, I was designed for pleasure, and what I wanted definitely would make me feel that. The voice had been right. I took what I wanted, and for a time I had exactly what I expected. But the pleasure did not last long, but the memory of it, well it drove me to desire even more.

In my youth, I was viewed as a handsome man. I was tall, standing more than a foot higher than most of the other men in my village and my muscles were well developed, allowing me to look like the Roman statues that dotted some of our larger towns. I knew my good looks and athletic build attracted many appreciative glances from the women, and envious stares from the men. I used my good fortune to fulfill many of my desires. I was often invited to parties, and I learned to appreciate the wine that was often served in abundance.

The voice was always there, helping me to experience what I wanted time and time again. I wondered why it never seemed to be enough, and why from time to time I would feel a pang of regret.

Even that first time when I gave into my desires, there was a much smaller voice warning me what I was doing was neither good for me—or right—but that voice was overwhelmed by the exuberance of the much louder voice. That smaller voice warned me what I was doing denied the truth that the woman I was with was made in the image of someone who would demand an accounting. I never considered what my actions said to the other person, after all, they all seemed to enjoy it as much as I did. When I enjoyed the wine, that small voice would return again expressing concern that I was losing control, but the louder voice became a cacophony of voices, all urging me to ignore that warning. I gladly did, as I wanted the feeling of success and pleasure that swept over me.

But that all changed after one particular party that ended in an all-night feast of pleasure. So many others were participating in the orgy I convinced myself it must be good. So many could not be wrong together, could they? It was during that experience I realized the smaller voice had not spoken, and it was then that the louder voices took control. Some of the things I did at that feast I had never considered doing. There was cheering all around me, as many stopped to watch, and even more jumped into the activities with me. I realized I was no longer in control. At one point in my mind I even cried out in fear as I recognized that I was destroying everything I had once held as important. But it was too late. The many now owned me.

After that event I ran. Everything in my mind told me to flee. I ended up in the caverns close to our village. I would spend many days there, sleeping little. The great care I had taken of my body fell away. Soon my beard and my hair were no longer neatly trimmed, and the clothes I wore became rags quickly. I learned to eat things I had never considered before. All types of insects were my feast now. Once, when I thought about returning to the village, the voices became so loud in my head I threw myself from one of the lips of a ravine, only to find myself at the bottom of the ravine, bruised and battered, but still alive. And the voices were laughing. My howling sounded exactly like what was coming from that herd of animals streaking away from my location.

Some of my friends and family came from the village. They cornered me and had brought chains with which to bind me. I know they intended good, but with my great strength I rent the chains asunder, and they all fled from me. One of the women I had been with brought baskets of food, leaving it for me. I did not understand her care. I recognized her as one of the ones whom the voices also claimed they owned. But when she came, the voices caused me to snarl at her, as if she were the enemy. She quickly withdrew, but it was one of the few times I was able to push the voices aside, and I ate what she brought. The food was wonderful, but then the cramps started, and within a little time all that I ate was vomited up. And the voices laughed.

Time had no meaning to me. How many months had I spent in the caverns, and how many nights had I roamed the hills? I was like the wild animals, and I often found myself screaming into the night. All I wanted was for the agony to cease, but whenever I thought such things, the voices would drive me to some injury. Until today.

I saw the woman who had brought the food to me—the one the voices had claimed they owned. But she was with a man who was followed by many other people. I was perched on one of the cliffs just above the ravines that led to the caverns, and I was watching. The voices began screaming, seeking to have me flee, but the man had called me using my name. The voices

185

could not overcome that call, and I ran to him, finding myself before him, and fell at his feet. The voices within me cried out, *"What do you want with me, Jesus, Son of the Most High God? I beg you, don't torture me!"*

"What is your name?" the man named Jesus asked.

Then I knew who had been in control for so long, and what happened next would change everything.

AUTHORS NOTES

Of all of Christ's miracles, other than his own resurrection, the raising of Lazarus from the dead is the most remarkable. I know there has been discussion on whether Lazarus's body had been kept from the corruption that Martha expected, which generated her caution about the odor which would certainly be present after four days in the tomb. Personally, I believe the corruption was there, but Jesus had the power not only to command Lazarus's spirit return to his earthly temple but also to reverse the very decay that marked Lazarus as unmistakably dead.

Jesus had already displayed similar power by the healing of lepers, who would often be marked by noticeable fleshly decay. And if He could command the waves and the wind to cease, and defy other normal physical realities, like walking on water, I believe it is more likely His command did more than just return Lazarus's spirit to his body. Then there is the whole scene of Jesus delaying returning to Bethany for several days after He received the note from Lazarus's sisters that "the one you love is sick." Jesus knew exactly what was happening to Lazarus and what He was going to do.

I find it remarkable that Jesus first speaks of Lazarus's death as "sleeping." Indeed, this language would be adopted elsewhere, where death would no longer be defined as "the end" but as an intermediate state, waiting for the great "awakening" of those who have fallen asleep. Death is still a terrible thing. Sin brought death into the creation where it did not belong. But that first sin also brought the great promise of the redemption.

That picture in Genesis of the gloating and

standing snake being indwelt by Satan is forever the picture we should remember when we consider death. Satan fully expected the extinction of man. He expected that God's justice would demand that lighting come out of the sky and return man to the dust from which he was formed. What Satan could not have foreseen or known was that God would offer man mercy when none had been offered to Satan. It is no accident that when God passes in front of Moses while hiding Moses in the cleft of the rock, the first attribute you hear him say is that of being merciful. Indeed, mankind is the single-greatest display of both the Love of God and His Mercy. Love and Mercy are intwined together, but not at the expense of His justice. Instead, His love and mercy provide the solution that fulfills His justice as well.

Indeed, the great promise of Genesis 3:15 is that One would come who would crush the head of Satan, but there would be a cost for that mercy. The One who would come to rescue man would be bruised by Satan.

Needless to say, most of us would pale if we really considered what that bruising would entail. Not only His rejection by the very people He had come to save, but the excruciating torture that preceded His execution by crucifixion and the abandonment of His closest friends at his time of greatest need, followed by His Father's pouring out of all of His wrath upon His only son. Christ's cry of "Why have you abandoned me?" by necessity precedes His final words, "It is finished."

Lazarus is a small glimpse into who Jesus really is.

I also found it amazing and difficult to grapple with, that unlike the blind man in John 9, whose voice is one of the clearest proclamations of who Jesus is, you never get to hear a single word from Lazarus's lips. You get to hear both of his sisters speak, as both

188

Martha and Mary have vocal parts in the gospels and in the stories. But Lazarus is quite quiet. I found myself asking why? The only answer I could come up with, is because the real story is not about Lazarus but about Jesus. It is fascinating to me, that just Lazarus being alive is enough to cause the leaders to seek his death as well. His existence after death needs no words. Just his being alive is testimony enough to scare the leaders into wanting him dead.

The scriptures do not tell us what happens to Lazarus and his sisters. So, some of what I have written about comes from the traditions passed down in the church over the generations. There really is a church in Cyprus that was constructed in the early 10th century over a crypt that dated from the 100s. A plaque on that crypt states, "Lazarus, four days dead, a friend of Christ."

Most of the relationships I have created come from my imagination. But what is not from my imagination is the fact that so many of these miracles, Simon the Leper, the healing of the blind man, and the resurrection of Lazarus, all occurred in that tiny village of Bethany, less than two miles from Jerusalem. I am confident these individuals all knew one another. In fact, the scriptures make that point evident. Martha is serving in the home of Simon the Leper, and it is in that home where Mary anoints Jesus, resulting in Judas trying to shame her. The miracle of the blind man given eyes is used by the people considering Lazarus's death and being critical that Jesus had given the blind man sight but had failed to prevent Lazarus's death.

For me, these miracles have played a significant role in the Lord drawing me to His person. It is my hope that the stories I have woven about these individuals will draw many back to the scriptures where the real stories exist. Any errors are mine; any who are drawn to Christ are His work. It is my hope to

189

know these people who were touched by Christ's power, and I look forward to returning with them when Jesus returns with all whom He has perfected and redeemed. I hope to see many of you in that gathering that is too large to number.

Grace and Peace,
Charles de Andrade

www.ingramcontent.com/pod-product-compliance
Lightning Source LLC
Chambersburg PA
CBHW071657290626
47170CB00019B/1589